the Tempest Within

the Tempest Within

GERI GODBOLT

The Tempest Within

Copyright © 2021 by Geri Godbolt. All rights reserved.

No part of this publication may be reproduced, stored in a retrieval system or transmitted in any way by any means, electronic, mechanical, photocopy, recording or otherwise without the prior permission of the author except as provided by USA copyright law.

The opinions expressed by the author are not necessarily those of URLink Print and Media.

1603 Capitol Ave., Suite 310 Cheyenne, Wyoming USA 82001
1-888-980-6523 | admin@urlinkpublishing.com

URLink Print and Media is committed to excellence in the publishing industry.

Book design copyright © 2021 by URLink Print and Media. All rights reserved.

Published in the United States of America
Library of Congress Control Number: 2021915863
ISBN 978-1-64753-903-0 (Paperback)
ISBN 978-1-64753-927-6 (Hardback)
ISBN 978-1-64753-904-7 (Digital)

23.06.21

CONTENTS

Introduction 7
Prologue 9
Chapter I   Chosen for the furnace of affliction 11
Chapter II   Tragically Finding Me! 27
Chapter III Wolf in Sheep Clothing 59
Chapter IV   Chattered Dreams and Broken Promises 73
Chapter V   Blind Trust 77

INTRODUCTION

I'm reminded of a time when boy and girl relationships were a matter of; "Do you like me, *yes* or *no*?" A simple cutesy kind of puppy love. Innocent and pure yet harnessing the reality of a mysterious foe called love. You find yourself playing with obliviousness because, once bitten you're never the same.

Love can sometimes be viewed as the enemy of our emotion if perverted by some adverse situations in which some sick-minded person uses it as a tool to conquer or as a tool to gain notches on their belt and/or build their sick ego merely due to lack of understanding, sheer ignorance, or narcissistic behavior.

Love the greatest thing that ever was and is. There is nothing more powerful than love. Even the bible states this fact. "*Faith, love, hope and charity but the greatest of these is love*". *{I Corinthians 13: 13;KJV}* God so "loved" the world that He gave his only begotten son, Jesus, the epitome of love. *{John 3: 16; KJV}* It is *He* who engulfed the essence of love because *He* is love on every level beyond our mere finite understanding. Also, *He* who teaches us how to love if we let Him; but that's another book, at another time on another subject.

King Solomon said, "*Set me as a seal upon thine heart, as a seal upon thine arms: for love is strong as death; jealousy is cruel as the grave: the coals thereof are coals of fire, which hath a most vehement flame. Many waters cannot quench love, neither can the floods drown it: if a man would give all the substance of his house for love, it would utterly be contemned.*"*{Song of Solomon 8: 6,7 KJV}*

Now he embraced the depths of an understanding of love far beyond most of our understanding of what love is or is about. The kind of love that causes two people to fit together like hand and glove making a snug fit where the two just melt into one the other not knowing where one begins and the other ends.

We have a tendency to love because of what someone does or does not do, sort of a cause an effect love. It's rare that you'll find unconditional love because it's easy to love someone that loves you back in the same way that you love him or her. It's easy when the person is easy to love. Love becomes hard when the person is difficult due to low self-esteem, domineering, controlling, insecure, over protective, needy, jealous, deceptive, self-centered, manipulative, sick due to physical, mood or mental disorders or just a jerk!

Let's deal with four different relationships involving one person all in the name of love causing an emotional tempest inside to rage and subside like a title wave in a raging sea, challenging their mental, spiritual and emotional state beyond most human limits.

PROLOGUE

***My name is Jewel and this is my story. The purpose of disclosing this information is to educate those of you who are seeking love on the misconception that it is easily obtained by all whom seek it. Some people have to pay a dear price for love.

Who said love was easy? Who fed you the lie? Who covers you when you have been beaten, raped, provoked, or tried by the man who stands behind the pulpit; or the God-fearing corporate giant, the leader of innocent lives; or the one who cares for patients daily and still nurses larvae for flies, sleeping in your bed nightly? He's the one whom everybody looks up to, whom we're never taught to hate. Who's playing charades? Who bore this man-child of deception and served him up on a platinum plate? He's the court jester with the crown. The Solomon whom everyone looks up to and desperately seeks out for help, advice, and care. While your eyes are focused on the kingdom, the tempest within is lying right next to the heir. Yes, your significant other, your husband and friend. The man whom you cover but clock your own deep scars in sin.

CHAPTER

I

Chosen for the furnace of affliction

Upon returning to my hometown, Philadelphia, I was approached at church by a former admirer of my early teens, Guy Stevenson. I call him an admirer because my father forbid me to date him even though we were both members of the same church. My father said he was a city slicker and was not fit to date his daughter. When ever he would call the house my father would tell him he couldn't talk to me. One day he finally told him to never call his house again. Well, needless to say we later moved to Columbus, South Carolina not due to anything he had done; my dad just made a decision that it would be better for us if we moved after my mother and grandmother, (her mother), died. They both had been sick for quite some time, suffering from incurable diseases and passed the same year with in months of each other. My father thought it best that he be close to his family for the support he would now need to help raise three daughters two of whom were in their senior year of high school and the other in middle school. I on the other hand could not stomach the south and returned home right after I graduated. I applied for college in my home state and was accepted. The only catch was that I had to stay with my Uncle Stanley and aunt Dottie to make the cost of college more affordable for me to attend. I did not mind this arrangement because I got along with my uncle and aunt equally as well and it was good to be back home. So, I guess Guy took my return as a second chance for love. He wrote my name in his bible when we were young and said I would someday be his wife. He was determined that I was going to be his bride. I guess he forgot about courtship or finding out whether or not I was interested. Every time I entered the church there he was asking me out and my answer would always be the same; "No, I'm not interested in gong out with you." Soon he got the hint; so I thought.

After being back home a while I started dating a former boyfriend, Lynn Collins. Lynn was so sweet, mild natured and handsome. I believe it was the familiarity that we felt with each other that drew us back together. We went together for quite some time. This was Lynn's junior year of college. Lynn went away to college while I remained home attending a university in my hometown close to where I lived.

I also returned to my former church, the largest and most beautiful church in all of Philadelphia. Well, this is the way I felt. I was home sick remember! My pastor welcomed me with open arms. To my surprise he had never removed my families name from the membership roll. I was back into full swing after a few weeks, on every committee and auxiliary I was a part of before we moved. It was as if I had never left. I felt such peace and fulfillment being back around familiar surroundings. There were a few new faces but for the most part every thing was the same.

While attending choir rehearsal one Thursday evening I was told by some girl friends of mine that this particular young minister would watch me when I got out of my car as I walked from the parking lot to the church, every time I was on the church grounds. One day I noticed this young minister at the church stalking me it seemed. Everywhere I turned there he was staring with these dark deviant eyes. I tried my best to ignore him. He gave me this sick airy feeling which made me nervous to move around in the church alone.

I was very close to my Uncle Stanley and aunt Dottie they always told me that I could come to them and talk about anything. They told me to never hold anything inside, to always know that I could talk to them because they would always be there for me. I had taken all I could take from this minister whom I thought behavior was strange and inappropriate. Besides he was beginning to make me nervous to come to church. I told my uncle that a young minister was following me. He asked me to describe this young man. He said he would speak with him. The next day my uncle told me that this young man likes me and would like to ask me out. I told my uncle I didn't want to go out with this minister and to please inform him of this fact. My uncle just laughed and said okay. My uncle told me a few days later that he spoke with the young man and he said he just nodded his head. He also said the young minister asked him for a job. My uncle was a painter and owned a painting company. I asked my uncle if he gave him a job and my uncle replied, "Yes as a matter of fact I did." I looked at him as if he had lost his mind! I said, "Do you know what you have done?" My uncle said, "Girl that boy is not going to mess with you." I told my uncle to keep him away from me.

One evening when my uncle was dropping off some supplies at the house he had him in the car. He got out of the car and came in the house with my uncle. He had the coldest smirkish look on his face and starred at me with cold eyes. He said, "You think you're better than I am don't you?" "You think you're too good to go out with me." "Well, I'm going to get you so watch your back." Just then my uncle came from his office and asked what was wrong. There was such a cold chill in the room. He asked if everything was all right. The young minister quickly replied, "Yes, everything is just fine." "I was having a friendly talk with your niece. My uncle could see in my face that something was wrong. So, he told the young man to go to the car and wait for him. I told my uncle what he said and he laughed. He said, "That boy is just trying to scare you into going out with him. "I'll take care of it don't worry." "He is one of the nicest young men I know." "He respects me highly!" "Give him a chance baby he may not be so bad after all." I said, "I can't besides I'm seeing Lynn." My uncle replied, "Lynn is away at college and there is a lot of young ladies at school." "I told my uncle that Lynn knows better." We wrote each other every week. So, I knew pretty much what he would and would not do. Lynn was mild mannered and even-tempered. I had nothing to worry about with him. I felt it was time I had a serious talk with my aunt about this minister since my uncle didn't seem to be listening. Aunt Dottie told me to watch myself around him when my uncle brings him home on his stops between jobs. My aunt said she would speak with my uncle concerning this young man. She said, "I don't think you have much to worry about, after all he is a minister." "We'll watch him together baby, you and I and everything will be just fine." Things weren't fine as a matter of fact they got progressively worse.

One evening after he and my uncle finished an exhausting day working he somehow convinced my uncle that he could get a ride home from our house because he felt my uncle was too tired to take him home. He told my uncle that he had done more than enough for him already. He said he could at lease find a ride home from his house. He asked my uncle to let him use our phone to call his cousin to pick him up. My uncle consented and told him he was more than welcome to use the phone and to make himself at home. He said, "You're not a stranger." Uncle Stanley smiled and went to the kitchen where my aunt was setting the table for dinner. My uncle returned to the great room and asked the young minister to stay for dinner. The young minister, who by the way is named Josh, said he would stay and asked if he could call his cousin back so he could tell him to pick him up later. I guess I always refer to him as the young minister because I hate to say his name. My aunt asked if all of us were ready to eat and if so, dinner is now served. After dinner Josh kept telling my aunt how delicious dinner was; what an over kill. She smiled and continued to say thanks and you are always welcome to dinner. That was the worse thing she could have said because he ate with us more frequently. He wormed his way into my aunt's heart with much deceit and flattery.

When I came home one evening and found him in our house alone I asked him what was he doing in our house and where was my uncle. Josh said they would be back shortly they went to the store. He then asked me if I was afraid to be alone with him or was I just fighting the feeling. I told him to go to hell. I told him that "you may be able to fool my aunt and uncle but you don't fool me." By that time my uncle pulled up and they got out of the car and came in the house. My aunt later apologized for my having to come home and find Josh in the house alone. She said she didn't think about me returning home from work. She said because he makes me feel uncomfortable she would see to it that that not happen again. Somehow I felt that it was too late for that. He had already begun casing the house. He became too comfortable with the surroundings.

One evening after dinner I told my aunt I was going to lay down to take a nap. I wasn't feeling well and seemed to be very tired that day. It seemed as if the children at work wore me out. I worked with the inner city youth program teaching reading through the S.A.R. program and tutoring after school each day to help supplement my college expenses. I graded papers and went to bed. I remember putting on a football jersey. I always sleep in big shirts. I find them very comfortable. I woke up later to find my aunt and uncle gone and the house dark. I guess they forgot to leave any lights on as they were leaving the house. Most people do that so they won't return to a dark house. I don't know what they were thinking at the time. I turned the light on in the hallway so I could see my way down the stairs. As I reached the bottom I spotted a note with my name on the front setting upright on the cadenza in the foyer that my aunt and uncle had left saying they had gone to the movies. I thought it very strange that they would leave a note and not leave one light on. I knew they weren't that backwards, although, they did have some strange ways at times.

I was thirsty so I went to the kitchen and looked in the refrigerator to get something to drink. I didn't bother to turn the kitchen light on because I didn't plan on staying down stairs long and the refrigerator light seemed to serve the purpose just fine. All of a sudden I felt this airy feeling come over me. I got shaky and decided to ease out of the kitchen and return back upstairs to my bedroom. This was my first thought. It never played out that way because that demon minister Josh was lurking in the shadows watching my every move. He obviously slipped into the house or never left when my uncle and aunt left for the movies. He gave such a nasty laugh when he saw that he had startled me. I was really frightened far beyond the effects of just being startled. This twisted demented psycho was in my house and there was know telling what was on his mind. I didn't see a knife, broom, hammer, wrench, screwdriver, or mop. I just wanted something to knock this fool slam out! He had something in his hand and I couldn't see exactly what it was because I was afraid to turn completely around to get a good look. He said, "I told you I would get you". I stood there in silence trying to think about my next move. I thought my best bet would be to act as if he didn't frighten me at all and turn around and face him. This monster was ahead of the game.

He studied me as if he was reviewing notes for final exams. He knew I was bold enough to confront him thus gaining the upper hand of this terrifying situation. He knew I would never succumb to his will. If I could only see what he was holding so I could gage the distance between him and myself. Then I could get a good grip on the glass I was holding in my hand and could smash it into his face. This was a fantasy compared to what this sick fool had already planned in that twisted mind of his. I was literally stuck between the open door of the refrigerator and open space in this dark kitchen. I felt so helpless and at the same time stupid for not turning on the light in the kitchen when I first went in. Then I got angry and said to him, "you stupid son of a demented sea biscuit". You better get out of this house. That just got him heated. He grabbed my head from behind never giving me the chance to turn around and face him. He put a sharp object to my neck and told me to put the glass in the refrigerator. I told Josh to stop this because my aunt and uncle had been too good to him and this would break their heart if they knew he was this twisted (*trying to appeal to his softer side*). He just laughed and said; "This doesn't have anything to do with them". He didn't move that object from my neck until he took me to the living room and cuffed me to the chair. This was an oversized high back chair. He cuffed my arms to the legs of the chair and my feet to the legs of the love seat so they would be in a spread eagle position. This was very heavy old Chippendale furniture.

He gagged my mouth with a rag and scarf. The object he held was a straight razor and he repeatedly reminded me that he would use it if I tried anything funny. Josh had already had the handcuffs in place on the legs of the furniture. It was apparent that he had been planning this for a while. He was just waiting for his opportune time to carry it out. My tears and squirming movement excited him to the point of arousal. He told me that my tears would be my own lubrication so keep crying missy. Believe me, I didn't just stand there and let this fool bound me. I tried to fight and struggled to get away, that is when he kept threatening my life if I did anything funny. My thoughts were dear God please get me out of here alive. 'He said,"you thought you were too good for me missy". "Well, look at you now". "Who has the upper hand now"? He began to rub his hands over his genitals and grab himself through his pants and moan. He said, "This baby has wanted you since the first time I laid eyes on you". "Now it's going to get its treat". He reached his hand under my shirt and ripped off my underwear. Josh looked at my private parts as if he was in a candy factory. He began licking his lips like a craved starved dog chasing a female dog in heat. He said, "Sweet and innocent, the best kind righteous, clean, tight and serene". "This has never been touched and if so, rarely". "Well, I'm going to fix it so no one can ever enjoy this pleasure". "You call yourself saving yourself for that college boyfriend of yours but when I get finish missy he'll have to find the pieces. I could feel his venomous hatred as he stared back and forth from my private parts and my tear filled eyes. He proceeded to take his hands and run them over my breast, down my abdomen and thighs while laughing to himself and telling me this is going to be a night you'll never forget. He rammed his fingers into my private scraping the inner walls as he pulled them out. He laughed harder as I tried screaming and squirming for him to stop. He kept plunging his fingers in and scraping the inner walls as he pulled them out until my private parts was a bloody mess. He then said while running his hand cover with blood over his genitals, "Now you're just right for this baby to get what it wants, good and wet like I like it."

    He was a sick prick. This low-life trash drove his ghastly tool so deep into my womb I could feel it ripping even worse than it had already been torn by his fingers. I felt as if my womb had been torn apart into pieces and this is what he wanted me to feel. He said,

"I couldn't take any chances on not getting in missy." "This is the tightest stuff I have taken in a long time." He continued to plunge in and out until he climaxed. That wasn't enough for him. This sick twisted demon played with himself until he got erect again and drove it into my rectum, releasing my bowel onto the floor and called me a dirty b...... He said I shouldn't have done that to my uncle's floor. So, he wiped it up into his hand and rubbed it all over my face and body, then licked it up like a thirsty dog lapping water. Afterwards he plunged himself still covered with blood, semen and bowel back into my womb, in and out fiercely, which drove him into a violent rage. I was in so much pain at this time; I wished I could have just passed out to relieve the agony of this awful torment. I was too mad to want to die; instead I wanted him to pay dearly.

He finally begin to feel himself climax and pulled out of my womb then begin rubbing himself vigorously while squirting his filthy sperm all over my me. This scum bag took his nasty hands and rubbed his wet filth all over my face, then slapped my face with the back of his hand and said, "now, I took what you thought was too precious to give up." "Now you don't have anything left to save for your prince missy." He kicked me in the stomach before removing the handcuffs from my arms and legs. This demented prick grabbed my head and bashed it against the leg of the chair so hard I felt as if my head was exploding and I passed out.

When I came to, my aunt was on her knees crying beside me. I guess they must have come in shortly after he left. My uncle couldn't look at me. He asked my aunt to clean me up, but she said, "The police needs to be called first." My uncle said, "Who did she say did this horrible thing?" My aunt asked me, "Who did this Jewel?" I said, "Josh." My aunt fell back and screamed at my uncle; "She tried to tell you but you wouldn't listen!" He said, "How was I to know he would do this?" My uncle said we, "can't call the police, there'll be a big scandal behind this and we will never live it down." "Everyone will say we let this happen to her." "You understand baby?" "Besides it's wrong for us to call the police on a fellow brother in the church." "The bible speaks of not going to the law on a brother, instead we are to bring him before the elders of the church." "I'll have to think about it for a spell." "In the mean time don't mention this to anyone." "Now please get her up and take her up stairs and clean her up." My uncle told my aunt to let him know when she had finished so he could explain things and pray with me. My aunt looked at me with tears streaming down her face. She struggled to lift me. She told my uncle as painful as it may be you are going to have to help me get her upstairs. "She's a bloody mess and we are not doctors and we do not know how badly damaged she is." He became frustrated with my aunt and glared at her with hurtful eyes and said, well, we know how to pray that God keeps her until I can finger this out." "Now go run her a nice warm bath so this sin can be washed from her."

When aunt Dottie came back down stairs my Uncle Stanley lifted me up very carefully and said, "This would not have happened if you would have treated Josh nice and given him a chance like I told you." My aunt became even more discussed with him but dared not say any more. My uncle sat me on the commode and left out of the bathroom. Aunt Dottie held me tight in her arms and said, "My dear child, I'm so sorry this thing has happened to you." "I can't explain all of your uncle's reasons but I know he's looking out for your best interest." "You see baby, it's hard to go after a minister in the church." "Who would believe us?" "Let me clean you up first, and then I'll help you get in bed so you can get some rest." "When you wake up you'll feel better." After my aunt finished washing me from head to toe, all accept my private parts, she handed me the washcloth and told me to think past what has happened and wash myself real good to get rid of the sin. She said this would help a lot. I became nauseated and threw up all on the side of the tub. Aunt Dottie cleaned it up and lifted me out of the tub while asking me to help her by trying to lift myself while she was lifting me. My whole body was numb. I felt as if I had been betrayed by my aunt and uncle to save this sick psycho who calls himself a minister. Once my aunt dried me off she helped me get into clean clothes and then into bed. I couldn't feel anything because everything that I felt was safe had betrayed me.

My aunt said she had to let Uncle Stanley know I was ready for him to come upstairs without even asking me if it was okay. Neither one of them asked me how I felt, where did it hurt, nor what happened? They just thought about what people in the church would think about them, not me, them! Uncle Stanley walked into the room slowly staring at the floor the whole time. I thought this was so cowardly of him. Yet I felt so sorry for him that he was so weak and timid not being able to stand up for what would be the right thing to do on my behalf. This is when I begin disliking weak men. The sight of my uncle began to make me sick. I sat in silence staring at him with pure discuss. His every word sickened me even more. He told me that I should call off work for a few days and miss a couple of days of school. He said a few days of rest should give me back some of my strength and by next weekend we'll go to church and not speak a word to anyone. He said some things are best kept inside. He said in time this well pass and my body is strong enough to heal itself because I'm young. I couldn't stop the tears from flowing down my face. I believe I cried everyday that week.

We went to church the next Sunday as my uncle had planned. I could barely walk. I went back to school and work even though I felt as if my insides were going to fall out with every movement I made. My condition worsened instead of getting better. My uncle made me promise that I would never say anything to anyone. He said this would destroy the family. I never answered him. I became weaker and weaker, by end of the month I was so sick I could barely stand. While in church the following Sunday, this would be the first Sunday of the following month, our pastor called me forward for prayer. Pastor said I had been on his mind. He said he could look at me and tell something was wrong. After he prayed for me he told me he wanted to see me in his office after church. I agreed to see him. I needed someone to talk to about this horrifying experience.

Finally the service ended and I went into the Pastor's office as I had agreed. He looked at me and said what is wrong. Pastor had known me since I was a young girl. My return had only made his heart glad. He was in many ways a father I never had. He said he could tell something was wrong with me for some time now and was hoping I would come to him. I told him I wanted to but my uncle asked me to promise not to tell anyone what had happened to me. Pastor said he didn't understand and ask me to start from the beginning. I did and when I got to the part about Josh raping me and told in every detail what he had done. Pastor became outraged with not only Josh and his psychotic behavior but with my uncle and aunt as well. He sent for both of them to come in the office immediately. I never saw Pastor so furious. He demanded that my uncle explain his actions toward this matter at once. He asked him what was he thinking not notifying him so the matter could have been handled properly and safer for me. I got sick all over again. I really thought that he was going to ask him why he didn't notify the police. Pastor never mentioned the police. My aunt told Pastor that she told my uncle to call the police but he refused. She also told him that my uncle said this would cause a scandal. Pastor agreed with that much of what my uncle had done and said he was upset that he didn't contact him immediately.

I felt as if someone had put a dagger in my heart. I felt even more betrayed. I trusted this man like a daughter trust her father and looked at him for many years as my father. I trusted him with my life; after all he was the watchman over my soul. I had to trust he knew what was best for me. How could the man of God I've known all my life, my Pastor, not want the very best for me? I was so confused and yet sick with despair. I felt alone, deserted, and frightened. I asked myself if I had done something wrong. I knew in my heart that I hadn't, but needed some answers as to how these people I love and trust could be so insensitive to what had taken place with me.

Pastor started making plans at once to have me examined. He contacted a doctor he knew with a clinic; of course this doctor was an obstetrician and gynecologist with a private clinic. I was to see him the next day in the evening of course. Pastor wanted it that way and so did my uncle and aunt so that no one could find out. The doctor promised not to ever report this to the proper authorities. Pastor said he knew I was hurt by all of this, but to trust that he was doing the best thing for me first and foremost, then for everyone else affected by this. He said God would see to it that Josh pays for his sin and that he would deal with Josh personally. Pastor silenced him for a while and removed him from the pulpit to the front row but he still had to dress in his ministerial clothing and was required to perform his other ministerial duties.

The next evening I arrived at the clinic to be examined by the doctor. He asked me to urinate into a cup so he could perform a pregnancy test. I went into the rest room and did as he asked but with much discomfort. It was very painful for me to pass urine. When I came out of the rest room I handed the cup covered with a paper towel to the doctor. He asked me to undress and get onto an examining table in this large room full of a lot of equipment and instruments. He was as gentle as he could possibly be considering all that had taken place. He asked me to please try and relax while he took a look. His expression on his face spoke volumes before he verbalized his thoughts. "Oh my God!" He said these words with such discuss. He said, "How could someone be so sick." He said there was extensive damage done and that I was pregnant from this ordeal but could not possibly think of keeping this child because I would never be able to carry it full term and live. He said one way or the other I could not keep this baby and live.

He spoke with my uncle and aunt after asking me if I wanted them to know what he had found. I consented to him speaking to my uncle, aunt and Pastor. He said I had a terrible infection from the deep lacerations, bruises and inflammation in my womb. He told them that my hemorrhoids looked as if they had been torn out of my rectum and left to hang out and rot. The doctor said my rectum was badly torn and also infected. He said it looked as if a crazed animal had tried to rip my insides out. I told him the church does not allow abortions and I held the same belief. He called my Pastor and told him his intentions. My Pastor convinced him to let me go for the evening so he could have a chance to speak with me. The doctor said he would need time to treat the infections first so I had a few days before he would perform the procedure. He said I was too weak as well and didn't see how I made it this long without help. Little did he know that I prayed for my life everyday. I asked God to keep me alive and let someone help me.

My aunt cried all the way home and my uncle never uttered a word. He helped me out of the car and suddenly looked at me with tear filled eyes and said, "I didn't know what to do sweet heart." "We've never been here before", like I had; Give me a break! I looked at him with tears streaming down my face and spoke with much discuss and said, "I've never been here before either and I've never felt more betrayed." He said, "I'm so sorry Jewel."

The next morning the phone rang; it was Pastor he asked my uncle to bring me to his office at the church so he could talk to me. They treated me as if I was an object, not a person. Why couldn't he have asked for me and told me to come to his office himself? I was sick of them talking around me, about me and not to me. Pastor hugged me when I arrived at his office. He signaled my uncle to leave and asked me to have a seat. As I sat he closed his eyes because it hurt him to see me in so much pain. It hurt to sit or stand so I just did the best I could to get around. I knew I wasn't going to stop going to school and it was an absolute fact that I needed to continue working in order to support myself. Besides my uncle made me go on as if nothing had ever occurred. He was in serious denial and wallowing in a pool of guilt. Nevertheless we had to co-exist in this house because I had nowhere else to go.

As I found a comfortable position in the chair I looked at the pastor as if he was a man I was having a formal meeting with for the first time. I no longer felt as if I knew this man. He became a stranger to me. I was skeptical of his every gesture and word. I took every word with a grain of salt and question his genuine sincerity. The pastor look puzzled for a spell. He didn't know what was going through my mind, but he knew there was something wrong between us. He asked me if I trusted him. I said, "I did before I heard your response after you found out what this disgusting sick freak had done to me." "You treated this as if it were something you could put a band aid on and it would just go away in a few days if ignored." "You asked me what was wrong but never how I felt or what I wanted to do." "The only thing that seemed important to you, my uncle and aunt was making sure no one ever finds out because of the scandal it would bring to the church."

Pastor sat back in his chair and stared at me for a moment and then leaned forward clutching his hands together on his desk. He said, "You are very important to me Jewel and you will never cease being my daughter in the Lord." I've known you sense you were a little young girl." "You are a very special part of this ministry." "Whatever I do at this point is for your better good." "I know you don't understand my actions or the stand the church takes in these matters, but it is most important to me that you understand that I really love you and care about your total welfare." "I'm doing what's best for you Jewel." "You must believe this!" "Trust me." "Have I ever failed you as a pastor?" I had no other choice than to reply; "No!" Pastor said, "Well, then trust me." "I will not fail you now." "Later on in life you will be glad I handled things in this matter; besides we do not take our brother to court we handle these matters in the church."

"Some people are born for the furnace of affliction, you are one of them and you will be able to help someone else through this experience." He said, "This didn't happen to you for no reason." "There is a purpose for all of the things that are taking place in your life." He said, "You don't see it now, but one day you'll be able to see and know the purpose." Pastor said, "Trust God to take care of this matter Jewel." I said, "Okay." I knew I could trust God because I purposed not to cease from praying until God vindicated me and dealt with that demented freak, Josh. I wanted this whole ordeal over with. I didn't want to bring shame on the church, my uncle, aunt or myself. I just wanted to know I was pleasing God and being obedient in complying with the wishes of my elders. Pastor said in this case it was not wrong to have an abortion because this was a matter of life or death and the seed was spoiled. He said it was a bad seed. I agreed to have him set up my appointment with the doctor in his private clinic. Pastor said we must keep this private and no one must ever know what has taken place.

That next week I arrived at the doctor's private clinic. Needless to say, I was very nervous. My palms were sweaty; I couldn't speak a word for fear of crying and never being able to stop. I felt as if I was having a nervous break down. I felt myself go numb when the doctor told my aunt to have a seat in the waiting room and directed me into the same room with all of the equipment and instruments I was in when he first examined me. The only difference was a large machine with a hose attached to it. It reminded me of an old antiquated vacuum cleaner. To tell the truth at the time the machine seem to be this monstrous object I described but I later found out it was much smaller.

The doctor asked me to undress and gave me a hospital gown to put on and left the room. When he thought I was ready he knocked on the door and entered with a pleasant smile on his face. He said, "I'm not gong to be to long and this shouldn't be too painful because I'm going to give you a local anesthetic." He said I would feel some discomfort but if all goes well it will only be for a short period of time. He said he was certain that the antibiotics he had prescribed had taken care of the infections. He said after the abortion he would have to repair the damage done on the inside of my womb and rectum. He made sure he had some antibiotics dripping into my veins during the procedures due to my having a mitral valve prolapse and to treat any infection on the on set of any occurring. It seemed as if I was attached every way but loose. He made sure he covered all grounds and his butt!

When the doctor began the procedure I felt confident in knowing God was with me no matter how nervous I was. Whatever it was that he gave me made my body relax and go numb. All of a sudden with out warning I felt as if something was sucking my very insides out. My body began to tremble with fear. It seemed as if something had gone wrong and fear seemed to evade, snatching what little confidence I had. I felt as if I was going to die and this doctor was the one to finish the job Josh had started. At that moment I felt as if a plot had been set against my total existence and all of them, my uncle, aunt, pastor, Josh and the doctor had got together and planned my demise so I would never utter a word of this to anyone. I began to panic as my mind wondered causing my imagination to sore into trip mode. I became delusional with panic.

The doctor told me to relax this will only take a few minutes. He seemed to have distant himself from my emotional state. He was only concerned with completing the procedures he was scheduled to perform. I really believe he upped the dosage of whatever it was that he gave me originally for my body to relax and go numb because my body relaxed slowly causing a calming effect. When he finished sucking my insides out, really performing the actual abortion, he said he was now ready to begin repairing the other damage. He was finally finished and asked me if I was okay. I just nodded my head. I was too weak to speak. He told my aunt she could come and sit with me for an hour and then if I was doing well I could go home and straight to bed. He prescribed medicine for pain and inflammation as well as an antibiotic to fight off any infection. He said I would need bed rest for the rest of the week and to return to his office the following week.

The days ahead were rough and my body took its time healing but all went well. God took care of me. In all of this I lost Lynn. I forgot to tell you that he was the pastor's son and after all I was now tarnished. I couldn't be angry with him he was just following instructions. We remained tight friends because we really cared about each other. I don't know what he was told and we never discussed it.

Josh just continued to get into more trouble. He never left the church but started dating a young girl outside of the church and got her pregnant and tried to stomp the baby out of her. This girl and her family weren't members of our church or any other church, so they had his butt arrested. Someone posted bail for him. A member of our church son tragically murdered Josh after he teased and badgered him in front of a crowd of people and kept hitting him while laughing, calling him a faget. The news said the boy pulled out a knife and stabbed Josh repeatedly. He died in an alley cursing and wallowing in his own pool of blood before he could be tried for almost killing that young girl and their baby.

I can't look at this as God's vengeance because I believe God gave him a space and time to repent and get himself together but he refused. I will say this; Josh died the way he lived. I believe what took place with him was self-destruction and his own self-inflected demise became my vindication.

CHAPTER

II

Tragically Finding Me!

I continued attending church and my relationship with the pastor was getting back on track. I forgave my uncle and aunt because they were in many ways just as devastated as I was with what had taken place. There are some lines you learn as a child to never cross.

Well, you remember the young man, Guy; I mentioned that was so desperately in love with me, and everywhere I turned there he was in church lurking in the shadows; he didn't get the picture. He was even more determined I was going to be his wife since he now knew Lynn and I were no longer dating. He was just waiting for the opportune time to make his move. Every time the doors of the church opened there he was with this slight grin on his face gazing and ever so gently speaking; "Hello Jewel." "How are you today?" He was persistent, I'll give him that much, but a pest in every sense of the word.

One day after work my aunt told me pastor wanted me to call his office. I called and pastor said, "Hi sugar bless you, I was waiting on your call." "Is everything, alright?" I said, "Yes." Pastor said, "How was your day at school and work?" I said, "Fine." By this time I was puzzled to find out what was really on his mind. He generally would check on me when he saw me at church or call periodically throughout the week in conversation with my uncle and aunt. Although he would ask to speak with me as well, I knew this was not a routine check up to find out about my well-being. I allowed him to continue general conversation as I wondered what the ulterior motive of this call was really about. I knew him well enough to know he had something else on his agenda for me. I could feel it. I just didn't know what it was.

Pastor asked me if I would come to his office from work the next day. I said yes. I was curious to find out what he had on his mind. That night all kind of thoughts ran through my mind. I was hoping he was going to tell me that Lynn and I could begin seeing one another again. I missed Lynn and he expressed the same when he wrote. Maybe it would be as if this nightmare had never happened after all! Lynn and I could be together as we planned. I soon drifted off to sleep after praying for God to reveal the truth concerning pastor's call today when I go in to see him tomorrow after work.

I arrived at pastor's office as I promised, greeted by the most pleasant secretary in the entire world, Mrs. Terry. She knew how to make everyone that entered pastors office feel important. She always left you with a feeling of self-worth. I believe she was given a special ministry of greeting people if this makes any sense. I smiled at her and told her she made my day. Mrs. Terry laughed and said, "That's what I'm here for."

I opened the door to pastor's office after Mrs. Terry informed him I had arrived. He was setting there with this child like grin on his face and began asking the same questions as he did the day before but this time after I reassured him I was doing fine I asked him what did he really want to see me about. I told him I could feel on the phone yesterday he had more on his mind than a routine check up on my well-being. He laughed and said, "You know your pastor to well Jewel." "As a matter of fact I do have something I want to talk to you about." I smiled in hopes it would be his consent for Lynn and I to be together. I sat there with great anticipation waiting for the words I so much wanted to hear to fall from his lips. He pulled out a letter from his desk and opened it and told me he would like to read it to me with the permission of the person that wrote it. Obviously he and this person had spoken prior to our meeting and this was what this meeting was about. Well, I asked God to reveal the truth. I still was hoping it was Lynn's letter. After all I hadn't done anything wrong why should I be punished. The horrible ordeal was over with and it was time for my life to take a new direction. My physical and spiritual healing wasn't enough I needed to heal emotionally and mentally. I needed to know it was okay to be loved genuinely by a human being.

I leaned forward as I was setting in this beautiful accent chair in pastor's office. While rubbing the arm of the chair with my right hand I gazed at my hand and asked pastor if the letter was from Lynn. I looked up waiting for his response. He slowly replied, "No." My heart sank. I stopped rubbing the arm of the chair and began tapping it with my fingernails and asked him who wrote this letter. He asked if I would let him read the letter first he would then tell me who wrote it. I said. "Okay, pastor read the letter." "I'm sorry for interrupting you."

As he began reading the letter I stopped him again and asked if he could give me a hint. He just laughed and said, "you'll know in time please let me read." Again I apologized and told him to go ahead. I was very puzzled as to who could this mysterious person be. I tried setting calmly until I finally relaxed putting my wondering mind to rest. Just listen I told myself in silent thought, you'll know in a few minutes. He asked me was I ready for him to begin again? I said, "Yes, please." "I won't interrupt you this time."

He began reading:

Dear Pastor,

I'm writing you this letter to express my feelings about this young lady I have loved since my early teens. I believe God has sent her back to be my wife. I knew very early that she was the one for me. I really love her pastor and she loves me too. I need your permission for us to wed. I really want to marry her, no fooling! Jewel knows we are met to be together she's just confused about all of this because it happened so fast. I spoke with her concerning us getting together with you in order to begin wedding plans. Pastor

THE TEMPEST WITHIN

Jewel makes me happier than anyone I've ever dated. I know this is meant to be. Please give us your blessings. I love her no fooling. Guy

I looked at pastor in disbelief. I could not believe what I had just heard. Were my ears deceiving me? Was this really happening or was this a nightmare that I needed to escape? Did he say Guy? Why couldn't I just wake up and move on as if this conversation had never taken place? Had I become too relaxed from the calm state I place my mind in, in order to be able to listen to pastor read this letter and slipped into a state of delusional rest? Had I just lost my mind? What had just taken place? Was I just played by Guy? Was this one of the reasons Lynn stop dating me? This farce of a letter hanging over our relationship triggered his distant response toward me? How long was pastor holding this letter? Did he read this to Lynn? After all he was his son. My God, what is happening to me? At first these thought were running so rapid they had my mind racing a hundred miles a minute. I was speechless with dismay. I was too through! Guy sounded so convincing he almost convinced me I had uttered those things he spoke of in his letter. I tried my best to swallow but my mouth was so dry it seemed as if my saliva had evaporated from my being. I managed to clear my throat as dry and empty as it was so I could speak to pastor in my own defense.

"Pastor," I said struggling with every word. "I did not say those things Guy wrote. I don't know where this letter came from or why he would write such lies. Every time he tried to ask me out I refused." "I don't know why he would write such lies to you." "We never spoke of marriage because we never dated." "You know who I love." "I don't even like Guy let alone love or want to marry him." "You know me; I do not want Guy!"

I sat back and closed my eyes because I was so discussed with what Guy had done. It made me see that he would go to whatever lengths to get what he wanted. Pastor said, "Jewel look at me." "Why would Guy write a lie and then say I could read it in front of you?" I said, "Because he knew what it took to convince you and to get what he wanted." I said, "So you think I'm lying to you?" "You posed this question to me before when you wanted me to trust you." "You asked me if you've ever lied to me and I replied, no." "Well, now I'm asking you to trust me." "Have I ever lied to you?" Pastor looked at me and said, "No Jewel." Pastor looked down at his desk before taking a deep breath and said. "Jewel I believe Guy is God's choice for you, regardless of the extreme measures he took to get to you." "I believe this should let you see all the more how much he really loves you." "I believe you will make him an excellent wife." "He needs a strong wife by his side." "I believe this is God's number one choice for you and you'll make a fine couple." "Guy is a fine minister and he's destined to be an A-Number One Pastor." "You'll make a wonderful pastor's wife." "He has a great future and he is stable."

Guy's uncle was the Presiding Bishop of our state. His family was very prominent, very wealthy and held the key to all of the ministers', elders' and pastors' futures in the state; you get the picture. Pastor said, "Jewel this is God speaking not me." "This is God's will for you." "Do this and you won't go wrong." "You don't love him now but you'll grow to love him." With tears streaming down my face I said, "okay pastor, I'll do it if you believe it is God's will for my life." I was nineteen soon to be twenty in the next two months and all I wanted to do was please God. I didn't want to do anything in any way that would put me out of his perfect will for my life. I didn't know what his will was for me at this time, that's why I had a pastor, for direction.

I left pastor's office feeling as if I had accepted an enormous challenge. I thought I must write Lynn and tell him what really took place just incase someone had already informed him of this dreadful letter. I wanted him to read my words first and also tell him that I loved him but must do God's will according to what pastor had instructed. I had all kinds of mixed emotions warring inside of me. I didn't love this man. I didn't even like this man. I thought he was kind of acey decey. All of his friends or I should say most of his friends were homosexuals or had strong tendencies to be gay. I didn't want to be married to a man that didn't know who or what he was. Every time you saw Guy there came Scottie with all of his make up on his face, press to the tee. Well, both of them could dress but Guy didn't wear make up. That didn't matter there was something about Guy that just turned me off. Oh God, I thought, is this really what you want for me. I thought it must be, Pastor would never make up something to fit God's will based on his opinion, never.

    I was setting in my uncle's favorite chair one Saturday afternoon watching re-runs of *The Three Stooges* while my uncle was lying on the couch supposedly resting his eyes. He was really fast asleep but you would never get him to admit this. Although every time these three silly men did something funny he would laugh along with me and start back snoring when I stopped laughing along with the television audience. I didn't know whom I was laughing at more, them or my uncle. I laughed one time until tears were literally rolling down my cheeks. My side began to hurt they had me laughing so hard I could no longer set straight in the chair. I was having my own private party that afternoon being entertained by my uncle with his spontaneous spurts of laughter between lapse of snoring and the "Three Stooges" acting as foolish as ever. I needed this more than I knew. You know it is written, *"Laughter doeth good like medicine."* Well, that afternoon I had my fair share of laughter's medicine.

    The doorbell rang as I was trying to gain some semblance of composure. I went to the door trying to hold back the chuckles I was suppressing inside me. It was Guy. Well, guess what the chuckles ceased. He was the secret antidote and didn't even know it. I asked him what he wanted and he said, "You're not going to let me in Jewel?" I said, "No after the awful lies you told pastor." He said, "What are you talking about?" With a smirkish grin on his face and that sly yet goofy acting Scottie shadowing him. "Pastor said that your visit with him went well and that I shouldn't drag my feet asking you out Jewel." "So there, I came to ask you out." I told Guy I wasn't going anywhere with him and his sidekick Scottie. I told Guy the next time you come to ask me out on a date you come alone and maybe my answer will change. I knew I had to be obedient in doing what pastor spoke but Scottie was not a part of God's said will. I said God's said will because

    I didn't feel in my heart this was the right thing for me to do. Yet, at the same time I really didn't know God's will whether perfect or submissive that's why I had the man of God to direct me. This is what I was always taught and believed. He's the watchman for our souls. I wasn't going against the grain, not now. I knew obedience was better than sacrifice no matter what the sacrifice became; In this case I was the sacrifice. I could feel it but couldn't prove it at this time. I just had a gut feeling. This wasn't enough to convince anyone of my elders. By my elders I mean my uncle, aunt, and pastor. My girl friends even wanted me to marry him. They said he is the most eligible bachelor in Philadelphia and that I should feel like the luckiest girl in the world. They asked me if something was wrong with me. They said, "Girl do you know how wealthy he is?" None of this mattered to me, besides my family wasn't piss poor and pitiful. We did have a pot to pee in and a window to throw it out, if you get my drift. In other words he wasn't doing me any favors wanting to marry me. Well, I decided to go back and finish watching the *Three Stooges* so I could erase all of these thoughts from my mind and the image of Guy and his shadow sidekick Scottie from my sight.

As I was about to settle into position in the chair my aunt called me to the kitchen. She told me she needed to talk to me about my behavior towards Guy. I asked her what had I done or said wrong to him. She said, "Jewel you can win more bees with honey than you can with constant bitterness." I said, "Aunt Dottie I don't like Guy and it's hard to pretend that I do." I told her he might be a nice friend but he hasn't given me the chance to find out because of what he has done in forcing me to marry him." She said, "He's not forcing you Jewel." "He just knows what he wants and that just happens to be to marry you." "You know they always get what they want." "This is a privilege Jewel." "You should feel honored he chose you." She told me that while I was out there being snappy at him pastor called to see if he had come by to ask me out. She said she told pastor yes and that I snapped him in two when I saw Scottie with him and that I also told him not to visit me with his sidekick, Scottie. She said the pastor got quiet and hung up after saying good-bye. I told aunt Dottie I don't mean to make things uncomfortable for her and Uncle Stanley. I just need time to get use to the idea. She said, "You don't love him now but at lease respect his position and in time you'll grow to love him." *This is Jewel talking; "Believe me if anyone tells you this run!" "This is most definitely not true." "I just didn't know it at the time and had no one to tell me differently." "Oh my!" "Let me stop." "I'm about to give away to much information before I finish telling my story."* I said, "Okay aunt Dottie, when Guy comes over again I'll try my best to be pleasant." She smiled and said, "I knew I could count on you."

As expected the next day the door dell rang again and again it was Guy Stevenson. He started coming over regularly. Even sometimes unexpectedly he would show up as if we had all became his possession. He was ever so pleasing and ready to do most anything. Too perfect if you will, Mr. Johnny on the spot! Always wanting to buy or spend or do something to please. What was it that he was really hiding, I always asked myself? I have to admit his act was good. He had all of us convinced to some degree. Although sometimes he was overbearing, no one would dare to say anything for fear of hurting his feelings. There wasn't anything he wouldn't do for me and it seemed as if he would go to great lengths to please me. Something about him wasn't right because I still had these questions about him. There was a few times when I had to put him in his place but he seemed to handle it well. We would talk and everything seemed okay. I began to adjust myself to the idea of being married to him. I felt there was no way out of this anyway so I best get with the program.

We dated for a year and in that year I saw a lot of things that I was feeling that made me know there was something not quite right with Guy. I still had so many questions until one day I went to Pastor and begged him not to make me marry this man. Pastor let me sob and when I finished sobbing he said, "Jewel you're just afraid of what to expect your wedding night." I said, "No pastor I'm not in love with him and I have all of these questions still racing inside of me." "I know this isn't right for me." He said, "How do you know?" I said, "I just know." Pastor told me that everything was already planned and that it was too late to change plans. He said I would be okay. I left and went home to tell my aunt but she wouldn't listen. I called my sister and she told me not to marry him, not for the reasons I had suggested, she didn't like him. Then she said she spent too much money on her dress so I better marry him or someone. We both laughed.

I must say his mother didn't agree with it either, not because of me. It wasn't about me. She knew her son and knew he wasn't ready for marriage. She said a lot of things about him getting married, sometimes too much. She talked too much and was too attached to him and too much into his business, personal and other wise. Mother Stevenson was very domineering and controlling over her family, especially Guy. He seemed to like it when it fit his purpose but despised it when it went against what he wanted. She would say to me, "baby you're not blind to the truth and don't let anyone make you see differently." She would say these things in front of Guy and he would tell pastor. This would make pastor real upset and he would tell me not to listen to her nonsense. I would soon come to find out that everything she said wasn't always nonsense. Mother Stevenson didn't reveal the total truth about her son only what she wanted me to see. Although I really don't believe she knew his deepest dark secrets. I do know one thing; a leopard never changes its spots. I couldn't prove any of the things I was feeling. I knew they were so because I have this gift that I know God gave me at an early age. I can read people and situations, sometimes I get it in parts, (bits and pieces), or in full. It frightens me at times. I don't talk about it because I don't believe it's something to take lightly and most of the times I'll see and not say anything just pray. I think that's best. I will say something when I feel it's going to affect some ones life. It's not like I see all of the time because I don't. Sometimes God will reveal things and other times he won't. I have to pray and ask him to reveal the truth about a matter and he has never failed to reveal the truth whether I speak about it or not, when I pray this prayer he always reveal the truth one-way or the other. Well, even though I had already seen some things concerning Guy I knew I couldn't speak of them because no one would believe these things about Guy or were they just covering his butt and using me to do it! I continued to pray that God would make all things concerning Guy known to me.

My wedding day was fast approaching and I was exhausted from all of the preparation. This was to be the grandest wedding ever held in our church and believe me it was. I had a winter wonderland wedding. My gown was trimmed in marabou fur and my headpiece was all marabou fur. I carried a marabou fur muff with a bouquet attached trailing to the floor and my train was so long I had to have two little girls carry it. I wore antique satin slippers trimmed with marabou fur. I had sixteen bridesmaids, eight junior bridesmaids, maid of honor, matron of honor, and two flower girls, mock bride and groom, ring bearer, groomsmen, ushers, armor bearers and acolytes. There were so many imported flowers and customized arrangements to depict a winter wonderland it all made the church so beautiful. It was a candle light ceremony. The Bishop walked down in his garb and all others that followed according to protocol. You would have thought he was a king I was to be his queen. Believe me when I tell you this was all show. I cried when I picked my gown up at the wedding shop, when I was getting dressed at church in the dressing room and again at the alter. I was a teary eyed mess going to the alter! I did not want to marry this man. *"I was clearly being forced to and made to believe this was God's will." "I know this now but didn't know it then."* When pastor pronounced us husband and wife and directed us to kiss, I couldn't. He tried to kiss me but I couldn't see myself letting him put his tongue in my mouth. I really couldn't kiss this man. At the reception all I could think about was what would this night bring. I had to go home with this man and sleep with him. It made me sick to think of him touching me but I knew I had to do what was required of a wife. My body cringed of the thought of letting him touch me. The reception went well. Everything was so beautiful and there were so many gifts. We had some of the brothers in the church help carry them home. Guy took care of the honeymoon plans. He told me he was going to surprise me for our honeymoon so I didn't ask where we were going. I just got in the limousine and smiled, while inside my being I was sick with apprehension. Those questions would not go away no matter how much I tried to not think on them.

We arrived home and Guy got out and opened my door and helped me in the house. I smiled and told him thank you. He kissed me on the cheek and went back outside to help the men bring in all of our gifts. To my surprise Scottie came inside and sat on the sofa. I said, "I didn't know you were out there Scottie." He said, "You don't know a lot of things." He sounded like a jealous woman scorned. But, you know what? He was right. Guess what? There was no honeymoon ever planned by Guy. I or I should say we, myself, my uncle, aunt and pastor, who bought the cake as a gift, spent over thirty thousand dollars easily on this wedding and all of my furniture was setting in this house for both of us to enjoy and that didn't matter at first when I didn't know he hadn't planned our honeymoon. All of that changed because he didn't have to come out of his pocket for anything but his tucks. He could have at lease made plans for us to go on a honeymoon. Well, I tried to reason this frustration away by telling myself that maybe he was too ashamed to let me know he didn't have the money. Why didn't he have money? Well, maybe it was tied up. I stopped reasoning with myself and accepted the fact that there was no honeymoon to go on not now or ever. I walked through my beautiful home to the great room where the gifts were placed. I began reading the many cards and empting them of money. We also had a wishing well full of money. Guy told me to get all of the money out of the well and put it on his dresser. He said we would count it in the morning together. I said okay. Guy told me to come to him and he turned me around and unzipped my dress. I knew this meant he wanted to go to bed soon, so I thought. Maybe Guy planned a honeymoon at home. How sweet! Please, Guy told me he and Scottie his shadowing sidekick were going out for a while and don't wait up. He grabbed a key out of his tucks jacket pocket that looked like a hotel key and left. I was taught as a child never to ask a man where he was going when he leaves his home. Trust is the key, my mom would always say. Besides I don't have the time to chase, follow, check up on, or run anybody down. I believe grown people are just that, grown! Whatever is done in the dark will come to the light, nobody hides my grandmother would always say, nobody. I believed that then and still believe it to this day. I also believe in respect and Guy didn't show any, but that's something we will discuss when he gets back. This was our wedding night. Any other night would have been fine. I wasn't really upset because I didn't want him to touch me. I don't think he wanted to. He wanted Scottie it seemed.

I stayed up all night in my gown opening presents. I watched as the dawning of a new day broke through ushering in the sunshine like a ray of hope. It was a peaceful calming. I whispered a soft prayer of thanks to God for a new day and to help me face whatever challenge I met on this day. This would become my daily prayer. As I was leaving the great room I heard the front door open, Guy walked in with Scottie. Guy asked why I was still in my wedding gown. I said because I just sat in the great room and opened presents last night and didn't remove my gown. He looked at me and smiled and turned to Scottie and signaled him to leave and step in the room. Guy asked me if there was a problem or better yet did I have a problem. I said, "no and yes." "I don't have a personal problem but I do have a problem with you just coming in the house and not being here on our wedding night." Guy said, "Is that all?" "I thought something was wrong." He turned and walked away and went in the room with Scottie. Scottie looked at me and said, "Smile wedding girl." He had so much make up on his face you could scrape it off with a knife. This was clearly not the time to have words with Guy, he had an audience and I don't believe in making a scene in front of people. I went in the bedroom and took off my gown and took a shower. I put on a pair of slacks and shirt because I knew my family would be by to say good-bye before they left to return to Columbus, South Carolina. I went into the kitchen and got a garbage bag and put my gown and all of the accessories including my shoes in it.

When my family arrived I asked them to please take me with them. My sister laughed and asked was he too rough. I told her no because we didn't do anything. I told them he was out all night with Scottie. As I was talking Guy and Scottie walked in and my sister signaled for me to stop talking because she saw Guy enter the room before I did. Scottie came in and picked up my little niece and got make up all over her cute outfit. My sister asked him if he was wearing makeup and he said yes. I mean, who didn't know he was wearing makeup? You could see it a mile away! My sister was being sarcastic. My dad asked Guy was everything fine with us and he said, "Yes sir, never better." He said, "I felt bad last night because of the honeymoon thing and didn't want to upset Jewel so I stayed away." "I'm going to make it up to her." My dad just turned and walked away mumbling under his breath. He said let's go. Guy left the room and his sidekick followed. I begged my family not to leave me. "Please take me with you." My dad said let's see what he does first. To this day he wished he never uttered those words to me. I believe my dad may have spoken six words to Guy the whole time he was here for my wedding.

My family left and that began one of many days in hell that I would have to endure for many years to come. That day seemed to linger like a drugging migraine headache with no relief in sight. Guy felt the need to tell me he had a key, (*the same key I saw him put in his tuxedo pocket last night when he and Scottie left*), that a young lady gave him. It was a key to her hotel room. She wanted him to come and spend the night with her. He said he could have stayed but he decided not to because it was our wedding night and he and Scottie laughed. I told him that couldn't have meant too much to him because he didn't stay hear last night. Guy said he needed that night to get use to the idea of being married. I said, "You do that together I thought." Guy smiled and said, "Get over it, I'm here now." I told him I knew this was wrong in my heart but there was no way out. Guy said, "You'll get use to us being together Jewel, if it kills you or I; well; enough said." "Let's go to bed." I told Guy it's too early and I'm not sleepy. He said, "Aren't we suppose to consummate our wedding vows?" "Yes Jewel, so let's go to bed now." "Scottie shut the door on your way out." Scottie got up and said, "You could have at least asked me to leave nicely," while smiling at Guy. Scottie then said, "Don't hurt her too bad." "You got any Vaseline or that other stuff?" "I know K-Y Jelly!" Guy said, "I got this man." I was too mad to be embarrassed. I told Guy he should have more respect then to allow some man even if it is his friend to talk like that in front of me. Guy laughed and said,

"Loosen up Jewel." "He was only playing." Then Guy said, "don't spoil my moment Jewel." "Now let's go to bed."

We went into the bedroom and Guy began to unbutton my shirt. He had this serious look on his face and was breathing hard and fast. He told me to take my clothes off and get into bed. He took his clothes off and my eyes grew very large as I looked upon such large genitals. I thought I know he's not going to put that monster in me. It looked like a jumbo bat with two golf size balls attached. Good Lord! It was in full attention ready to perform upon command. His kiss was wet. I hate wet kisses. He was panting and breathing like a thirsty dog lapping water. Guy touched my breast for a hot second as if he didn't know what to do with them and then with out warning tried to penetrate my tight womb and became frustrated when he couldn't get it to go in. He was fumbling at first because he couldn't find the opening and when he found it he didn't seem to know how to put it in. I believe he was just as nervous as I was, but Guy had been with other women before. He had plenty of former girlfriends. I had seen pictures of them when he took me to his parent's house. Guy tried again and managed to get the tip slightly into the opening. I told Guy to be gentle and take his time and maybe it will go in. Guy said, "I know what I'm doing Jewel, let me handle this, okay?" I told Guy okay and laid there. "Guy it's hurting, please stop." He wouldn't stop he just kept pushing until he got it all in. Guy was groaning and growling like an ape. He became uncontrollably loud. He really was acting like an ape in the jungle. This was his party and I don't know where I was. I screamed at him to stop and then pushed at him to get off of me when he wouldn't, I told him to get off of me. I asked him what was wrong with him. I said, "You don't know what to do with a woman do you?" Guy began to cry and told me to shut the hell up. I was crying too because I was so sore from him constantly ramming the giant tool of his in and out of me and he thought we were making love. I said, "Guy I didn't mean to make you cry." "I just couldn't take any more of whatever it was you thought you were doing." He most definitely was heavily endowed. He needed a real woman I wasn't the one cut out for this job. I was just a young twenty one year old girl with no experience and no clue as to what I should do with all of what he was packing. He was very aggressive in bed like an untamed animal. No I wasn't a virgin but I still had no experience. I knew I had to get with the plan because I had made a vow with this man and it was my duty as his wife. I prayed that evening for God to help me go through this marriage and teach me how to make love to my husband so he could in turn learn how to make love to me. I also vowed to never turn my husband away again. *"I really didn't know what I had prayed and vowed at the time."*

I soon began to learn marriage is a ministry by way of giving life to someone through kindness, love, patience, long suffering, endurance, forbearance, trust, security, submission, humbleness, temperance, and strength; most importantly God's mercy and grace for each day. Grace and mercy became my best friends immediately. The next morning I slipped out of bed quietly so I wouldn't disturb Guy's sleep. I looked back as I was going into the bathroom to assure myself that I hadn't disturbed him. Guy was lying on his side of the bed wide-awake. I said good morning and Guy just stared at me with such a disgusting look of dislike and disappointment. Guy said he should have gone with the young lady who offered him to stay at her hotel room. He said maybe he didn't do the right thing by turning her down. I asked him why didn't he follow his heart and his response was, "What heart?" "Is this a heartfelt thing?" I looked at him and asked, "Why did you want to marry me so bad Guy that you lied and schemed to get me?" Guy said, "Because I always get what I want and I've wanted you for a long time." "I proved your dad wrong didn't I?" "You see Jewel; I'm good, real good." I turned away and started walking into the bathroom when Guy said, "Jewel I love you." "I just have to figure out how much." I stared at him and silently told him that I was going to shower. As the hot water was running down my body I began to think of how I could have handled the situation better last night and again I came to the same conclusion that I had done the best I could with what I was faced with. Maybe I could try again this morning and Guy wouldn't feel so bad about his performance. I hurried my shower along so I could catch Guy before he got out of bed. I put on lotion and some mild soft smelling perfume, Red. I brushed my teeth again and gargled for a whole minute. I knew I was nervous because my gums were bleeding due to my brushing my teeth so much that moment. The mouthwash burned so bad it had my eyes watering or were they watering from the fear of what I was about to challenge myself to endure. I put my housecoat on and walked back into our bedroom. Guy was still lying in bed. I walked over to his side of the bed and opened my housecoat and placed his hand on my breast and asked him to go freshen up and maybe we could try again. Guy smiled and said okay. Guy took a while in the bathroom but I waited since I felt guilty about my behavior last night. When Guy came out of the bathroom he had this big smile on his face. I was lying on his side of the bed so he would feel as if I was waiting desperately for him. He reached down and kissed me gently. I thought, Wow! Maybe he thought about his actions last night and felt just as bad as I was feeling. Guy snatched the pillow from under my head and began to smother me. I squirmed and reached upward; I put my claws in him and dug in and downward ripping his flesh like a wild animal in rage. I was in a fight for my life. All I could think about at this time was what that crazy Josh had already done to me. I had vowed if I could help it, this would never happen to me again. My heart was pounding ninety miles a minute. I thought, what had happened between the time Guy had gone into the bathroom and came out? Guy yelled out at me and called me crazy. He said he was just playing and wanted to put some excitement into it. He said he was teaching me a lesson as well. He told me to never push him off of me again because if he really wanted me last night he would have just taken it and there would have been nothing I could have done because I was his wife. I had scratched his shoulder badly but I didn't care. I sat up so I could catch my breath. When I could breathe I reached for my housecoat and Guy snatched it out of my hand and said, "Oh you're going to complete what you started Jewel." "You're not getting off that easy." "You need to be taught a lesson." "My uncle said sometimes women have to be taught a lesson and you won't have any more problems in that area again." *Remember Guy's uncle was our presiding Bishop and he believed his word to be gospel.* I told Guy to get out of my way and let me out of this bed. Guy saw how serious I was and said, "Jewel I'm sorry about trying to smother you." "It won't happen again but all of this excitement has got me …… well, you know and now you have to take care of me." "It's your duty Jewel, fix me, now." Guy said that is why some wives are lying in their graves now because of what they did to the man of God. I remembered my prayer from last night and wanted to take it back but I knew it would be wrong. I also felt this was wrong of Guy to expect me to be with him after the stunt he just pulled. Guy looked at me and said sternly, "Now Jewel." "I'm not waiting." My body cringed as I laid there and let Guy have what he wanted. It was no different from last night but I just let him finish so I could get this over with. I got up to go wash and tried hiding the tears streaming down my face and Guy pulled me back and said, "next time Jewel I'll take it." I said, "You just did." Guy smiled.

I went into the bathroom and took another shower and Guy got into the shower with me stating he didn't want to waste water. He told me to get over the drama. He said I would get use to him soon enough and asked me what were my plans for the day. I said I had none because I took off work thinking we were going on a honeymoon. Guy said, "Jewel you're having your honeymoon now." He said, "I'll take you to dinner this evening." I'm going out for a while and will be back later. "Oh, Jewel you can forget about going back to work too." "No wife of mine will work." I told Guy we didn't discuss this before hand and I like having my own money and I want to do my part as well. Guy smiled and said sarcastically, "Oh how cute of you Jewel but that was a given when you married me." Do you see any other woman in my family that is married to any of my uncles working?" "Jewel does my mother work?" I said, No but I'm sure they discussed it first." Guy said, "Jewel you'll find out that some things in this family are just not open for discussion. "Well, Guy I feel that this is something we need to discuss because you're not going to tell me whether I will continue to work or not without first talking things over with me and seeing if it is an option I would agree with. Guy look at me as if I had just cursed him out and said, "Jewel let's get this straight, you will never decide what will take place in my home." "You will do what I say." "I'm the head of this house." "God placed me as the head of this house and you will summit." "You need to understand God's plan of order for the home." "Jewel if I thought for a second you were being smart mouth we me I would knock the hell out of you, but I'm not because I realize you are just ignorant to some of the things of God." "I'll just have to show you what I mean because if you walk out of that door next week thinking you're going to work I'll come to the job and embarrass you and then bring you home." "Wait a minute Jewel, if you so much as get up to get dressed for work I'll strip you naked and…….. Well, I don't need to go any further you get the picture." "Let's just say you won't feel like walking not to mention going to work." "Don't try me Jewel." "Just stay sweet and submissive, we'll get along just fine." "Now if you're through testing my patience I'm leaving and will be back later." Guy left before I could respond to his last remarks rolling his eyes and slamming the door.

I was beyond furious; I was ready to slay my enemy. I really felt that Guy was my worst enemy and I was trapped inside this house to be tormented as an example of how the torment of hell is for those that don't make heaven; a constant reminder of a place where I did not what to go. Guy had more than an identity problem. This man was emotionally and mentally sick, I thought as I walked into the kitchen. He's clearly a typical Dr. Jeckle and Mr. Hyde jerk or is it more serious than that. I didn't know what to think but I knew my gut instinct was right about him from the beginning. I just can't but a label on it yet. Who would believe me concerning Guy? He's the church prince after all and who would have touched him even if they knew he was like this from the beginning, before we married. Maybe this is why they wanted to marry him off. Pastor said I was a strong young lady when he first spoke of Guy and I getting together that afternoon in his office a year ago and that was what Guy really needed, a strong woman beside him. Lord help me puke! I want to puke! A strong woman, he needs an exorcist for his exorcism. I need a quick deliverance from this mess I've been forced into. I found myself back on my knees asking God to reveal to me his purpose in all of this and asking him to give me strength to stand. I felt a peace and warm calm come over me as I knelt on the living room floor that felt like an angle guarding, covering me with it's wings, or ones mother tucking a child in with a freshly heated wool blanket for warmth and comfort, an assurance of security and rest in the one I knew loved and cared for me.

Guy came home later that evening as he said he would and we got all dressed up to go out to dinner. We both looked good if I must say so myself. We were one good-looking couple I thought to myself for a moment and sighed with a smile while looking up at Guy. He said, "What?" Why are you smiling Jewel?" I said, because we look good together." Guy said, I do make you look good don't I?" I said, What ever and laughed." Guy asked me to go to the car and wait for him. He said he would be out in a moment. I thought maybe things would work out after all. We had a great time that evening. Guy had made reservations at one of the most prestigious restaurants in Philadelphia. I felt like a queen. Guy even apologized to me for what had taken place earlier that day and for all that he had said that upset me. He said he had not changed his mind about my working. Guy said he would rather I stayed home because he wanted to take care of me and wanted his wife to not want for anything. I told him I understood and accepted his apology and would remain at home as he request. He promised me that his threat didn't mean anything. He said he would never hurt me and trust him and know that he loves me more than I understand. That confused me, but I dare not let on, I just smiled and said, "I believe you Guy." Guy looked at me and said, "So that means you'll never mention working again Jewel." I told Guy that I must be honest with him and say what I'm really saying is that I'm not going to mention it for now. "I'll let it go for now." Guy looked at me very sternly and said, "Jewel this subject is closed." I didn't want to ruin a good evening so I said, "okay." I knew we had to go home and wasn't sure what might happen if I didn't agree with Guy. Guy smiled and said, "That's what I want to hear. Now eat your food I have some more surprises for you this evening.

When it was time to leave the restaurant Guy stood up and came over to me, he kissed me then helped pull my chair from the table and helped me up. He took on the role of the perfect gentleman. When outside he again helped me into the car. We drove home holding hands. Guy lifted me out of the car when we arrived home and carried me into the house. Thank God I only weighed 110 pounds or I believe we would have been in trouble. He told me to cover my eyes and carried me into our bedroom. Guy told me to uncover my eyes and to my delight there was a beautiful red velvet housecoat and matching slippers from Saks Fifth Avenue lying on the bed. I know it was from Saks because I admired it when we went shopping there before we were married. He told me to follow the trail of roses, which lead to the fireplace mantle in the formal living room. He instructed me to collect the roses as I went along the trail. My eyes lit up like a glistening prism as I gazed upon an open box with a diamond and pearl ring sparkling with brilliance. I was speechless! The tears of joy streamed down my face. I began to laugh as I thanked him. Guy said "no Jewel it is I who needs to thank you because you have given me so much more." Guy must have done all of this when he told me to go to the car and wait for him just as we were leaving for dinner. At that moment I thought, had I misjudged Guy after all? Or was this a glimpse of another personality he is now displaying and if so I hope he is locked into this one! I'm glad I prayed that afternoon.

Things were great for the next few months. Guy wasn't home most of the time, but when he was he would go out of his way to be nice and do nice things for me. He brought home a bouquet of wild flowers weekly. Guy left roses for special occasions. It was nothing to wake up to gold, pearl, or diamond necklace place on the pillow beside me where he should have been resting his head. Sometimes he would walk in with beautiful suits, dresses and all of the accessories to match including shoes and purses. Guy could dress a woman from head to toe and did not need instruction or assistance in so doing. He bought my stockings from Park Lane. He preferred silk stockings only and bought them by the boxes. He also bought my underwear. There were times when I would ask him to let me buy my personal things. He would only reply, "I know what I like to see you in and what type of sanitary napkins you should use. On one occasion he let a church member buy my underwear for him. She smiled when handing me the bags and said she hoped they fit. I was so embarrassed. I told the Pastor about this and ask him to speak with Guy because he wasn't hearing me. The Pastor told me to be grateful that I had a husband that wanted to do so much for me.

After a while Guy would take the starter out of the car so I couldn't leave the house. I was being held prisoner in my own house. I could only leave when Guy was taking me somewhere. He began to have a buyer come to the house so I could shop from my living room. This was a woman's dream come true! I never complained about shopping at home. I asked him repeatedly why he would take the starter out of the car. He said he was monitoring me. Guy said I had all I needed at home and had no need to leave.

One evening guy locked me in the closet because I wanted to go with him to a concert. He had already made plans to go with Lonnie. Lonnie was another Elder in our church and was as gay as they come. He was married to Jackie and she was known to be a recovering or should I say delivered lesbian. I don't know how or why they even got married. Lonnie was over our house 24/7. It made me sick. I somehow got out of the closet and wondered whom could I get to help me out of this mess. You see Guy bought me all of those things because he was never home with me. He was always out with one of the Elders or ladies from our church or one of our affiliate churches. I was always left alone. The only time I went out was to church or when he took me shopping. Guy even did all of the grocery shopping by himself. I started asking Guy to let me stay at his mother's because I knew he wouldn't refuse this request. I wish I had thought of this sooner. I made a habit of going to his mother's house and she enjoyed the company. She would teach me how to bake things Guy liked and tell me more about Guy's childhood. I knew how to pick her for information. This was my only defense besides prayer. Through her I learned a lot about Guy's past. I read between the lines when she would speak because I knew she would only reveal what she wanted me to known. She would be exposing herself if she revealed too much.

She never knew how much she revealed in what she wouldn't say. My psychology training was at work after all.

On one occasion Guy called his mother's house and asked to speak to me. He was panting and breathing hard as if someone or something had frightened him. I asked him what was wrong and he asked me to go into another room so his mother couldn't listen to our conversation. I did as he asked while thinking to myself; "What in the hell is wrong with this fool." I said, "What's wrong honey?" Guy said he had to lock himself in our bedroom to keep Lonnie off of him and asked me to come home. He said he needed me at home to protect him. I was stunned I couldn't respond. He got mad and yelled, "bitch did you hear me?" I became even more speechless and at the same time furious with anger over what he had just called me. I said, "I hope he splits you wide open" I told him, "You need to come clean with me and tell the truth about what really had taken place there."

I told him I was coming home but not to stay. I told Guy I couldn't take anymore name-calling and abuse from him. Guy apologized and said he was scared. He said Lonnie was angry with him. Guy said please come home.

When I arrived home I found Lonnie on the couch holding himself and crying. I asked Lonnie what happened and why he was crying. He said Guy was in denial and he knew why he was crying. He told me to ask my husband why he was crying. I asked Lonnie to leave. Lonnie told me he was staying because Guy invited him over and would be the one to ask him to leave. He said he doubted very seriously if that was going to happen. He said Guy don't want him to reveal his secret and rolled his eyes. I went to our bedroom and knocked on the door and told Guy to open the door. Guy was in the bedroom lying in the dark. I reached to turn on the light and Guy asked me not to turn it on and to set on the bed and hold him. Guy was shaking with fear. I asked him if there was something going on between him and Lonnie. Guy cried and said he was sorry. He said Scottie was mad at him as well and he couldn't take everyone being angry with him. I ask Guy to stop crying and help me make sense of the things he was saying to me. I asked Guy about the love letters I had found from Lonnie. I assured him I hadn't spoken to anyone about the letters. I told him I just went to God in prayer for him to reveal the truth. *I mumbled to myself the older people always said be careful what you pray for.* Guy said, "what did you say Jewel?" I told him I was thinking out loud and praying for understanding. I needed all the understanding I could get at this very moment. I had also received a letter from a younger girl at our church, the pastor's daughter. She was very graphic about her encounter with Guy and said he couldn't do anything for her because he couldn't handle her. She knew every mark on his body. She made sure I knew she wasn't lying. She was one among many of Guy's sexual exploits. I just kept all of this before God in prayer because I had no one to talk to about Guy. He was untouchable. He was the church prince. He held the keys to everyone's future. He was a pond on a chest board and didn't even realize it, how sad.

That night some of the truth would be revealed. I knew not all because Guy was the one telling the story. Narcissistic people only reveal the things that gratify them and things they feel victimized by. My God, I had a husband with multiple personalities, violent, narcissistic, confused, questionable, and a womanizer, yet vulnerable. Guy was a sad case for sore eyes. In the dark that night he answered my question about him and Lonnie and some of the others. Guy told what happened to him when he was five years old. The man told him to never tell anyone. The man continued molesting him for years while he was a helpless little boy. This man was his baby sitter and a member of his church. His mother trusted him with Guy. I felt so helpless at that moment because I didn't know what to say to Guy. I told him that if he would seek help I would be beside him every step of the way. I told him I would stay with him if he were willing to get help and work harder on our marriage. I told him I would be here for him and help him as well. We both went into the living room and asked Lonnie to leave. Lonnie asked us to please let him stay that night and he would leave tomorrow. It was late so we said okay. I was so numb I didn't know what response to give to either Lonnie or Guy. I turned to Guy and said let's get some sleep. I told Guy I couldn't let him touch me sense he had been with Lonnie that night. Guy told me he knew that and told me that was why he stayed away from me most of the times. He told me to lie beside him so he could go to sleep.

That night I prayed extra hard for grace and mercy to get me through this nightmare. I also prayed for wisdom to handle the days ahead. We were soon fast to sleep and it seemed as soon as we went to sleep it was time to get up. Guy and Lonnie spoke in private and Lonnie left afterwards telling us he was sorry and he would see me around at church. We sought counsel. Guy seemed to be doing well at first and then he became very distant. Guy stopped going to our counseling sessions and became more abusive. He began to stock me at night. He would stand over me and threaten my life.

One morning he pulled me out of the bed by my neck and began chocking and kicking me in my stomach. I had blood in my throat and bruises on my stomach. I screamed for help. At that time an Elder from our church was staying with us from time to time for my protection so Guy wouldn't jump on me as much. He was appointed by the pastor to protect me so no one would find out what was taking place in our home. The Elder came rushing into our bedroom and pulled Guy off of me. The Elder literally had to kick open the door to our bedroom to get in because Guy had it locked. This went on continuously for months. Guy only continued to get worse. One night I was watching the burning bed and Guy came home and asked me what I was watching. He told me to cut it off. He asked me if I was planning to do the same thing to him. I said don't push me. Guy began pacing the floor and screamed at me to turn that TV off. He charged at me and I was ironing his shirts while I was watching the movie. I told him I would sear his chest with the iron if he didn't stop. The Pastor called by some miracle and I told him what was happening. He asked me if the Elder was at our house that night and I said no. He told me to put Guy on the phone. He spoke with Guy and Guy said, "I was just playing with her and she took it the wrong way." Of course the Pastor believed him. I called the Elder and spoke with his wife and told her what had happened and asked her to tell him to come over and stay with us. I told her I was not going to be responsible for what

I will do if he puts his hands on me that night. The Elder soon arrived at our home and asked if I was all right, I told him yes. He then asked where Guy was. I told him guy was in the bedroom. The Elder found Guy in our master bath cradled around the commode like an infant with his eyes rolling around in his head. He called for the pastor and another elder to come over. When they arrived Pastor asked the elders to close my bedroom door. They stayed in there for at least an hour or more. When the door finally opened Pastor came out and then the elders. Guy was still in the room. Pastor asked me to find it in my heart to forgive Guy and go into the bedroom and comfort him. He said he needed me and hadn't any real understanding of what he had done. He asked if I would take hold of the wisdom and understanding God had placed in me as a wife and embrace Guy as never before. I said yes. Obviously this was bigger than I had imagined and know one was willing to tell me Guy's true problem.

We made it through the night miraculously with no other incidence. I was so tired when we woke up that morning I could hardly get out of the bed. Guy asked me to make love to him. I couldn't, but I knew if I didn't he would probably kill me for rejecting him. I said "Guy I'm so tired and weak from last night." I asked if we could make love later when we both felt more refreshed. Guy said "no" and told me to get back in bed and well, I can't say what he told me to do. He was not going to let me off the hook. Guy began to suck my breast as if he were a baby feeding from his mother's breast. He sucked my breast until they became sore and then bit it. I told him he was hurting me and to please stop. Guy looked at me and told me to let him cleanse himself through me. He told me to just let him have his way and allow him to do whatever it took for him to free himself. He had his hand around my neck at this time. I couldn't scream out for help for fear he might snap my neck. I know we were in bed for over two hours. Guy would "get off" and rest on top of me so I wouldn't get up and then start back again. There was so many variables to what he was doing I'm at a lost to explain what happened. Just say I was one wore out sister when he finished. He cried while performing all of the acts he put me through. I got a life worth of experience in this two-hour ordeal. I thought, could anyone live through such torment? I asked Guy when it seemed he could do no more, if I could please get up. Guy said yes while panting out of breath. I went into the bathroom to shower. The shower became my place to shed tears and hide. I couldn't let Guy know I was crying or he would slap me or tell the Pastor I was not complying with his wishes.

One day Guy caught me crying, he stripped my clothes off in front of company or should I say Guy's company, and drug me into the shower. I had just left the salon. Guy got jealous because the salon manager asked if I would pose for his hair book. He said he liked my beautiful long hair and asked if I would pose with the stylist for his upcoming book. I asked Guy and he said no and became upset saying that man just wanted me. I was so miserable. When I got out of the shower Guy was standing in the bathroom and told me to get back in the shower. He said I needed to wash him off. I said, "Guy please!" Guy just looked and said, "Jewel wash me off." I said okay. I got back into the shower and washed and dried Guy off. Guy said he was going out to play ball with the other elders at the church. I said I'll see you when you get back and he turned and pulled me to him and kissed me then left. I didn't know what to think. That night not ten minutes after Guy stepped out onto the basketball court his achilles tendon tore. They said he yelled out with great pain. They called the ambulance and Guy went to the hospital. Guy was told he had torn his achilles tendon and that he would need an operation to fix it. The doctor sent him home on crutches with his foot and ankle bandaged up. The elders told me what happened and Guy looked at me as if it were my fault. I had to wait on him hand and foot. We went to the doctor's office later that week and scheduled his operation. When the day arrived for his operation his mother and I was in his room comforting him and reassuring him that he would pull through this just fine. His doctor explained to him that he would have a limp after the procedure. Guy wasn't to please with this. He looked at me and said this is your entire fault. His mother told him to stop that and to stop blaming me for what happened to him. She said he made the choice to go out on that court and play ball not me. I told Guy to try and relax because he knew this operation would take eight hours and he needed his strength. Guy asked his mother to leave the room so we could have our privacy. Guy really didn't want his mother to hear what he was about to say to me. Guy told me that I hoped he would die and that I was just pretending to care and he couldn't stand me. He said the sex wasn't good and he was tired of me. He told me he hated me and if he made it through this surgery I would pay for this accident. He said I knew he didn't really want to go play ball that night. I told Guy I didn't know what he was thinking at the time. I told Guy it's the medicine that has you talking like this. I told him I prayed for him and that he would make it through the operation. I kissed him and he spit at me. I left him in the room alone at that point. I waited in the waiting room with his mother until the operation was over. The doctor came to the area where we were waiting and told us that everything had gone as planned. He said he should recover fine but have a slight limp. I thanked him and went to the recovery room to see Guy. When Guy woke up and saw me standing beside him he reached out and thanked me. He told me he loved me. His mother said she didn't know why I kept covering him. Guy looked at his mother with discuss. His mother told me she was going home since he was all right and that she would check on him when he went home. After three days in the hospital Guy returned home. Guy agreed that it would be best for him to stay in the upstairs guest suite. He was so humble. It was as if this had changed him. Maybe he felt like he had been given a second chance. Not on your life! The better Guy felt it seemed the worse he got. One day after I gather his dinner plate from the bed he told me to hand him his mail. I told Guy I had put it beside him in the bed. He said, "I didn't ask you where it was." I told you to give it to me. This is the way the Bishop, his uncle, treated his wife. I handed the mail to Guy and he through it down. He said I didn't hand it to him right. I told Guy it's on the bed and he'll have to get it himself and walked out of the room. As I was going down the hallway Guy came hopping on his crutches towards me. I proceeded to go to the stairs and Guy stopped and griped his crutch in his hand and knocked me down the stairs with his crutch. I tumbled down the stairs plates and all like a child's toy that had been tossed aside in play. I couldn't get up at first because I was dazed. I called the police and reported him. I had had enough. The police arrived and Guy was still at the top of the stairs. By this time the Elder had arrived and the police asked if he could take Guy somewhere else to spend the night. Needless to say I was in big trouble from the church for calling the police, but at the time I didn't care anymore. The Elder understood and told me I had done the right thing. The next day when the Elder brought Guy back home he told me guy had something he wanted to say. I turned to Guy an asked "what?" Guy said he was sorry and said he was wrong. He asked if I would let him stay if he promised to do right. I said yes. The Elder told Guy he would be staying as well. Guy agreed. One day after things calmed down while at church we were waiting for Guy to come out of the office so he could began preaching. I went back quietly and opened the door only to find Guy making out with the Pastor's eldest daughter. They were so deeply involved that they never knew I saw them or just didn't care. I closed the door quietly and told the church he would be out shortly. We just sang more songs and waited. Guy got on the pulpit as if nothing had taken place. He even spoke in his own tongues. I was discussed. She was on my same row smiling at him and had the nerve to smile at me. I just smiled back. I acted as dumb as the both of them. Guy continued with this behavior between himself and other women and then back to men and I had had all I could take. I had no way out because I was told it was a sin to divorce an Elder. So, I decided to kill myself. One night after he jumped out of our bed and decided to throw me out of it when I returned to work just to keep sane. Guy then turned the bed over on top of me. He could have killed me, but God spared my life. That wasn't enough he begun to stalk me again and this time it was worse. I called the police when he tried to kill me and I had to resort to getting two butcher knives to protect myself. The Elder stepped in between us and took Guy to the other room. When he came back to check on me he saw I was bleeding and my finger was hanging on by a thread. The Elder rushed me to the hospital. I told him on the way there that they were going to let Guy kill me. I asked what had I done in life that made me go through so much craziness. When I returned home from the hospital Guy was in the living room crying. He told me I was a crazy b….. and he would kill me next time. This time the Elder got upset and took Guy to the Pastor. The Elder told me that the Pastor went up one side of Guy and down the other. The next morning when Guy went to work and the Elder left to go home I went to the medicine cabinet and took out Guy's Pain bills he got after his operation. I prayed and asked God to forgive me but I needed to be free from this bondage and this was my only way out. The phone rang or had been ringing. I say this because my friend said she had kept calling me for thirty minutes to an hour. She said God laid me heavy on her heart. Tonya said she didn't know why but she knew she had to get to me right away. When I finally heard the ring I answered the phone. I was out of it. I was in another world so to speak. After all I was contemplating killing myself. Tonya told me in a very loving voice to stop whatever I had planned and to stay right where I was and she would be over. When Tonya arrived she said I was on the kitchen floor crying and dazed. She helped me up and called the Elder's wife. They took me to the Pastor. And told him that he had to do something. She said I was like a zombie. The Pastor said he wasn't aware of anything being wrong between Guy and me. He asked if I would write him a letter explaining everything that had taken place between us. The Elder's wife said, "Yeah, that's why my husband is staying over their house most nights to protect her." The Pastor said nothing. My staying with Guy assured his position to become Bishop. They wanted to split the state and Guy's uncle liked me. He would call me out at every convention to let everyone notice Guy and his wife. My staying with Guy I believe, helping them disguise his illness would get him in the Bishop's seat. Well it worked because he became Bishop and succeeded to split the state. I quietly and secretly wrote the letter I was asked to write. I didn't leave out anything and kept a copy to give to the District Attorney upon his request. He wanted to have the Bishop arrested along with Guy after this last episode. Guy tried to stomp my insides out, tackle me and then tried to throw me out the guest suite window. I fought like a crazy woman. He bragged to his friends about what he had done. I couldn't have the Bishop arrested so I told him I was leaving Guy and asking for a divorce. I was called a fool for leaving our house but I just wanted peace of mind. Guy and I had put equal amounts down to purchase our home. We put down twenty grand a piece to buy that home. It was custom built. Guy said he would burn the house up with me in it if I tried to put him out of the house. The Pastor asked me to hold off on any decision. He asked me to stay and think about what I was loosing by leaving Guy. He said to think about the shame I was bringing to the church by exposing Guy. He said to leave him would be the same as my exposing him before the saints. Guy said, "Jewel you covered me all these years why are you not willing to cover me now." I told Guy I couldn't just let him kill me. I told him I was allowing him to kill me by staying. He said, "I'll kill you if you leave." This was the risk I felt I would just have to take. I was in church one night and while sitting there praising God a still voice spoke to me and posed this question, "Why sit ye here and die?" I jumped up and began praising God like I had lost my mind. I was free to leave! I had been released! I felt like a load had been lifted. The next month my dad and niece came to visit. My dad being blind not to mention this being his first trip on an airplane came for a serious reason. He told me I didn't grow up like this and didn't have to stay in this contrary to what anyone else in the church believed. He told me to get out of this mess. After he left I began divorce procedures.

I had been in an accident a year earlier and was waiting to settle. I had to go on permanent sick leave due to the injuries I had suffered. My former supervisor told me that I had income protection insurance and that my policy from my auto insurance covered me as well and I was getting a check from the company. I worked for Insurance Company. Needless to say I was overjoyed! I continued to receive a paycheck. I received a settlement check from my insurance company and still had a settlement from the other party's insurance company to settle. I didn't understand at first why my supervisor had me take out so much insurance coverage. She just kept saying you never have enough insurance. I'm glad I listened to the voice of wisdom. When I first went to see this place I didn't have a dime to my name. Well, not enough to talk about. I just prayed and asked God for guidance and favor. Well, God granted me favor I signed the contract before I knew I had all this coverage. I just moved in faith because God reassured me He had me covered. I moved into a luxury penthouse condo with all the trimmings. All of my furniture was paid for with cash because God had blessed. I had my own money; God gave me everything I needed to move and everything I needed to be sustained. My Lawyer also made Guy pay alimony and their fees. I really didn't want anything from Guy, but my lawyer said I would be crazy not making him pay something. I just wanted to be free.

I continued therapy for about six months. I needed to become a whole person. I used therapy, lying on my face before God, and crying out for deliverance and direction for my life to begin my healing process. I stayed in the area for a year and had to move because Guy and the Bishop would not leave me alone. When I tried to attend another church in our area I was condemned. I went back to my church; the Bishop wanted me to attend while watching Guy do his thing, I couldn't. One of the Elders came to me and asked that I try with Guy again and I told the Bishop and he said, "When God delivers you out of the mouth of the lion you don't put your head back in his mouth." I knew this by now I just wanted to know what he thought. I also went to see him to let him know I was leaving. I needed to move. I needed a fresh start, a new beginning. I was stronger now. God was refreshing my being. I learned a valuable lesson in all of this; never, allow anyone to have total control over you. Your Pastor, Bishop and Elder are the watchmen for your soul but they do not have control over you. God releases that control to no one. Only God owns you and He gives you free choice to choose His divine ownership. You don't have to if you don't want to, but I choose Him again and again!

I also need to say that all men of God are not this unbalanced or controlling. There are some awesome men of God out here. They just come few and far between and are to be cherished by their spouse, family and church members for following the mandates of God.

I can breathe and I love it! I smile and it comes from within because I enjoy life, my own company, discovering who I am and exploring my purpose.

CHAPTER

III

Wolf in Sheep Clothing

I had moved to Texas and love it. This was a whole new experience for me. A new place, new faces, and a fresh start, I had it made. Houston was a wonderful place! I loved shopping at the Galleria and going to Galveston walking the beach. I often took trips to Sanantonio to enjoy the river walk. Texas was spoiling me. I attended the Covenant love church in Houston. What an awesome change. I knew this was the place for me. The ministry was life changing! I kept my distance because I wanted to observe more before I took the plunge for membership. I had become acquainted with the leadership of this church through fellowship with an awesome pastor of the affiliate church in Pennsylvania. The pastor there was and still is an awesome man of God. He and his wife are outstanding people. He could also sing and was on many praise and worship cds from this ministry. This was the church I was told to stop attending while in Pennsylvania. I received a word from that church before I stopped attending from one of the Elders from the mother or head church from Mobile Alabama. The elder told me that God was going to heal me. I suffered a bad spine injury in the auto accident I was in two years earlier and had to have six injections to my spine twice a month. My condition was getting worse that was also another reason I needed to move from

Pennsylvania. The weather was much too cold for me. Texas seemed to suit me well. I visited the doctor in Pennsylvania Twice a month. I would fly in see the doctor get my shots stay at my friend's house and leave. I didn't choose to visit on my trips there because they weren't pleasure trips. On one particular visit to the doctors he told me he would need to go into my back. He also informed me that it would be risky surgery. He had consulted with a team of doctors and they had come to the conclusion that this was much needed surgery and my only option for possible recovery. Now you know I didn't believe this because I was told that God was going to heal me and my spirit received it and I accepted this truth, so for me this was a done deal. I heard a still voice tell me to let him do it. I heard God speak into my spirit and tell me to let them perform the procedure. I didn't understand but I obeyed. I said, "God you said you would heal me." God reassured me that he was in control. I went back to my friend's house and told her I was to have surgery within the next few weeks and would have to stay in the hospital a while and convalesce at her house for a few days and they would arrange a special flight for me to go to my sister in South Carolina. You get the picture by now. Yes, I had to leave Texas and go to South Carolina. My dad asked that I come there so I could recover and my sister could help me with my recovery. I consented and left Texas. I knew God had a plan in all of this. I just had to trust Him. All went as planned. Although I didn't recover as they thought I would. My back got worse but I would not stop praising God. When I was on my back let me tell you I was on my back. When I could stand I rejoiced! I would praise God like a crazy woman! I attended my godfather's church. He was a Bishop and the pastor of the church. One day while at church my god-sister's kept smiling at me and told me they had to tell me something. My god-sister had married a wonderful preacher and he had a brother that liked me. He liked me many years before I came back to South Carolina while attending my last year of high school there. I was told he liked me then but I was not staying in South Carolina then and was adjusting to having to return. His father and mother told me at that time I would be their daughter-in-law someday. I just smiled because

I knew in the back of my mind what I had already planned when I graduated. I remember when word got back that I was marring Guy he and his brother called and asked that I not do it. None of us were ready for marriage at that time.

His bother told me after church that he always saw me as his sister-in-law and would be glad if his brother and I got together. When I say the brother was on the hunt, I mean the brother was on the hunt. None of them would let me rest. They were a wonderful family. I knew them well but this brother was not like his brothers. They were saved and he was not! His brother along with my god-sisters said he had changed and was saved. They said he too was married at one time and it didn't work but he had changed and was a different person. His mother said the same. He really was her heart. So, she would say anything to please him. He was very handsome, a man in every since of the word and had a wonderful personality. From time to time they would visit my godfather's church. Sometime his brother would preach at the church since he was married to his daughter. Jeffrey could preach. He was anointed and lived right and treated my god-sister like a queen. He had a good example to follow. His father was a good man. He passed some years earlier before I returned to South Carolina. They were the perfect wholesome upright Christian family. His mother was precious and we got along well. Everyone wanted us to date. I took it slow. I didn't want a relationship at the time. I was fine, living single and free. I didn't feel a need to be with anyone and didn't want to be with anyone at this time.

This rascal was persistent and so was his family. My sister thought it would be nice if I would give him a chance. She said, "He is a changed man, in church and living right." "What more do you want?" I said, "Proof!" He invited me to go to church with him and I consented. I watched as he presided over the service at his brother's church. I must say I was watching a changed man. He did well and I enjoyed the service. I agreed to come to church with him next Sunday evening because I was to sing in the choir at my godfather's church Sunday morning and asking to be excused by my god-sister Denise, was out if the question. I talked with my godfather and asked him what he thought of me dating Greg. He knew Greg since he was a baby in diapers. He knew his history and said he seems to be a changed man. He told me he didn't see anything wrong with it and just told me to continue to take it slow. I ask my dad and he told me he seemed better than that other thing I had. Greg was also an educated man. I just prayed for God's guidance in all of this.

I soon found out why his family was so persistent in getting us together. He was involved with someone ten or twelve years his senior. She was obsessed with him. From my understanding she took care of him. My god-sister Denise told me all of these things because she said I needed to know why everyone was pushing me to respond to his wanting to date me. She said they were trying to get rid of this older woman in his life. I thanked her and started distancing myself from all of them. When they asked why I didn't come around I didn't have to reply she did it for me. She told them she had told me the truth. Everyone was upset with her and kept trying to convince me that this was far from the truth. They said he had been trying to get rid of her, Gladys, before I returned and she would not take no for an answer. His family reassured me they would never put me in that position. He invited me to church again and Gladys was there. He said he asked her to come at his family's permission to resolve any questions I had. His brother asked that I stand and told me he was glad I was there and the whole church clapped. He asked that I sing with the choir and I agreed. We had a wonderful time. After church I was asked to come to the back of the church where this woman he had been dating was standing. His brothers and mother came back as well. Greg introduced me to Gladys and he told her I was his heart and that we were now dating and he had plans to marry me. I smiled and shook her hand and told her it was a pleasure to meet her. She stood there gazing at me and said, "you're very pretty, and it's nice meeting you." I could see she was hurt. I asked her if we could talk later in private. She nodded her response. I told her I would get with her on the time and place. I could feel her hurt. I needed her to know that I was just as shocked as she was to find her at church. I needed her to know I didn't need to have an assurance from her that he was no longer involved with her. He and his family had made that perfectly clear. *"I would soon find out that I would be treated in the same manner or worse."* I asked Greg to take me home. His mother wanted to know why I didn't want to come to the house for dinner. This is what everyone in his family did every Sunday. I told Greg I didn't feel comfortable after what had just taken place. All his mother would say is that Gladys would get over it and had to find out sooner or later that she didn't belong in that family. She said, "It wasn't intended to offend me in any way so come and eat with us, you're family." I told Greg to take me home and he took me to my house and left.

I didn't talk to him for two weeks. His mother wanted to have lunch. We went out and had a great time. She explained herself and asked that I please understand her position. She said she always wanted me as her daughter-in-law since the first time she met me. Her children referred to her as Mayme and she asked that I do the same. She didn't like me calling her Mother Johnson. I thanked her and called her Mayme. This was awkward for me because I didn't like calling her by her first name. I could never call my mother by her first name while she was living she would view it as disrespect and possibly slap my face. Everyone runs his or her family different. This woman ruled her family. She was and still is the "godmother" of this family, just like the "godfather" of the movies, only this is a church family.

Greg and I dated for a year and a half before I would consent to marry him. I loved him and was ready to be married to him. He was doing well in church and by me. He displayed much respect for my standards and his standards as a man of God. We prayed together, praised God together, laughed and had fun, and we were very comfortable with each other. There was still something pulling at me. On the night I consented to marry him he came to my house with ice cream. He knew I liked ice cream. He gave me the ice cream and said, "Treats for my sweetie." I opened the bag and said thanks. I didn't see my ring until I pulled my ice cream out of the bag. I screamed! He had given me a three-carrot emerald cut diamond. I was speechless. With tear filled eyes he told me how much he loved me and how much it meant to him for me to be his wife. I told him I would love to be his wife.

One night he told me he couldn't move in my home. I asked why. He said that his mother told him that a man should never move in a woman's house. He said that he had to get a house for us to move in. I thought this was crazy thinking. I had a beautiful home with a pool and didn't plan on moving out of it just yet. He said he already found a house and asked if I would go with him the next day and see it. The next day when we arrived at the house there was a realtor waiting to let us in. It was a very nice house. It was smaller than my house but nevertheless nice. I said maybe we should look at some other properties before deciding on this property. We did, but came back to this property. He needed my help in getting this property and that was okay. I didn't mind helping out. But just at that moment I heard a voice say, "My way of escape." I was puzzled and ignored the voice. *"Believe me I would soon come to regret that choice."* We took my furniture after selling my home and put it in our new home. I moved in there before we married. I was in there two weeks before our wedding. Some of my furniture had to be placed in storage. It turned out to be a beautiful place.

Our wedding day was fast approaching and we were both anxious. Greg would call me every night before I would go to bed to say goodnight. Well, our wedding day had arrived. Greg called me at least twenty times asking me if I would marry him. He said he wanted to make sure I wasn't going to back out. I asked him if there was a problem and was this what he was feeling. He said no and said he needed to know I really wanted to marry him. I reassured him I wanted nothing more than to marry him. We were married that day and everything turned out as planned. Maybe my fears were not real after all. I was so happy. We were both happy. We went to a beautiful hotel that night and had a wonderful time consummating our vowels. He made me feel so special. He took his time undressing himself and then me. He led me into the shower and washed me. I washed him off and he dried me with a warm towel. When I reached to dry him he said he would dry himself. He said this was my night. He said he wanted to love me. He was so gentle because "God had blessed him well," if you know what I mean. I hadn't been touched in years, not since my marriage to Guy. I wasn't nervous. I felt safe. He had a sweet gentle spirit. I hoped I could please him. He was patient and taught me how to make love to him. He showed me what pleased him by performing his needs on me. He taught me through show and tell. We had a nice honeymoon. No we didn't go anywhere but the hotel for a couple of days, but we enjoyed one another.

The next week we both returned to work. We were both educators and I also owned a salon. I was also a licensed Cosmetologist. I would teach during the day and after school I would go to my salon. There was just the two of us, most of the time he wasn't home. So it was good I had a life outside of our home. One night around twelve o'clock in the morning the phone range, I answered it and the woman on the phone disguised her voice and asked for Greg. It was a very bad disguise. She tried to sound like an old telephone operator. Greg asked who it was and I told him she refuses to give her identity. Greg got upset and took the phone. He left the bedroom. I over heard him tell this person to never call our home again. He asked her if she was crazy. He came in the room and slammed the phone down. I asked him if everything was all right. He said yes. He told me he was sorry about that and told me it was Gladys on the phone. I asked how she got our number. Greg said he didn't know. I told him our home number is unlisted so someone had to give it to her. He then asked me if I was trying to blame him for giving her the number. I told Greg I know no one in his family would give her our number. Greg told me to let it go and go to sleep. He said he handled it and would get to the bottom of it in the morning. Greg said he was not going to argue with me about Gladys. He pulled me closer to him and said go to sleep baby. When we woke up the next morning Greg asked me if I was okay. He said I don't want you leaving for work upset. I told him I was fine. I lied to him and myself. I wasn't fine. I just hid my true feelings.

A few days went by and that weekend Greg's mother came to the house. She was angry. She spoke with me briefly and told Greg to step in the living room. She went up one side of Greg and down the other. She asked Greg how long had this affair been going on. Mayme was getting louder by the minute. He told her he had been seeing her since we were dating. He said he had been staying with her off and on since the previous fall. I just dropped into the chair in the kitchen. He was having an affair with Gladys before we married! He had stayed with her the night before our wedding! This would explain why he kept calling to make sure I wasn't going to back out on him. Apparently she had threatened to call and tell me what was going on. How Mayme found out I don't know but nothing gets passed her. She told him he better straighten this mess out and told him I better be smiling the next time she saw me. She told me sorry for disturbing my home but she had to straighten her son out. I just looked in silence and watched her leave. Greg came in the kitchen and said he could explain. I asked him was she in my car before we got married. He said what difference does that make now. I told him he just answered the question. I asked him does he have her in my car now and to my surprise Greg said, "Yes, now are you satisfied?" He told me he had to get her out of his system and I wasn't making it easy. I asked what had I done. I told him I was in the blind here. He told me he knew and didn't mean what he said. He told me he said those things because I wouldn't let it go. Greg told me he was a fool and had the best person standing in front of him. He said I was the perfect wife. This became the thing he would say every time he messed up.

Greg started staying closer to home. We went out more and began doing things together. He asked that I not go to the salon every night after school. I agreed and it seemed as if we were getting closer. Late one night I was wakened by the smell of smoke. I reached over for Greg and he was not in bed. He must have gotten up after I fell asleep. He would hold me until I would fall asleep. I got up quietly. I didn't want Greg to here me. I walked toward the opened garage door. The door leading to the garage was usually closed. GREG WAS IN THE GARAGE SMOKING WEED! I got so angry. I asked him what was the point. How long was he hiding this behavior? Greg said, "Well, I don't have to hide it any more. Greg told me to take my "butt" to bed. He told me he didn't want to argue with me or take his frustration out on me. Greg told me he was tried of living his life to please his family and me. He said he didn't want to be saved. He said he loved his life and wanted someone that wanted the same thing he wanted. He asked me to please get out of his sight and go to bed. I went into the bedroom and closed the door. That night I cried myself to sleep. The next morning I asked Greg where do we go from here? Greg said, "Jewel I don't know." "I know I don't want to loose you." I got ready for work and when I came out Greg grabbed me and said let's play hooky today. I said okay and we both called off. We had to make sure we got substitutes for our classes; we found them and took the day off. I asked Greg what he had in mind. He said, "Can you just go with the flow?" "Do you always have to know what's taking place next?" I just told him I never had anyone teach me how to be married or how I should respond to my husband spontaneously. I asked him to teach me. He said before this is all said and done I will teach you more than you'll ever want to know. He asked me to ride over his friend Shana's house. I told him I wouldn't be comfortable at Shana's house because she was a Lesbian. Greg said, "She doesn't want you." "She knows I don't play that". Greg said to tell the truth she's really bisexual. He said when they get real high sometimes he'll tell her to give him a blowjob. Greg said he doesn't ask me because he knows I can't relate. Greg said, "If you are to remain my wife you will learn everything it takes to please me and really satisfy me." I told Greg I thought he was pleased. I told him I've tried to do what you asked and you seemed to be pleased. He said, "Jewel don't get me wrong you're a good girl the perfect wife and you do please me when I just want stay at home sex." He said, "You're tight, its right but sometimes I want you to get wild with me and that comes naturally baby, you don't have it."

I agreed to go with him to Shana's house and she seemed to be more nervous than I was that he had brought me. She asked if I wanted anything to drink and I declined. I believe I took advantage of her nervousness by controlling the conversation. That day I won over a friend and had a chance to witness. Needless to say Greg was upset things didn't go as he had planned. I really don't know what he had planned but I do know he was upset that his plans were shot to pot! I laughed within because this time I had beat this devil at his own game. He didn't realize every time he showed his behind I obtained a new lesson in life. He was a good teacher.

He started staying out more. He began using our house as a pit stop or a hotel, a place where he would come just to change. I began reading "He Came to Set the Captive Free" by Rebecca Brown MD. I just stayed on my face before God. I continued to praise God. I didn't talk out of my home. No one knew at first what was going on so I thought, until he became very public with his mess. He began to date other educators. He even went so far as to date a co-worker. They were so bold they walked the halls at school together. I asked him to leave our home. He told me he would leave when he got ready. His brothers stayed over our house because he would come home either drunk, high, or both. By this time he was on crack. High school girls were calling our house for him. Other women were calling our home and saying he told them I was his sister. I would come home at times and find blond hair in our bed. Sometimes he would come home so drunk and vomit all over the bed or just urinate and defecate on himself. I would have to clean him up and strip the bed. Every time he was sorry and I was the perfect wife. Between the alcohol, other women and drugs I don't know which was worse.

One day his car was in the shop and he had to use my car. This meant he had to take me to work first. He dropped me off and before I got out of the car he told me everyone knew he didn't want me. He said I was the only one that didn't know it. I said nothing. I got out and went into my classroom. One particular teacher he was dating would call me on a regular basis and ask me not to keep him home. He called them in front of me as if I didn't exist. In his mind I didn't. He told them we were two strangers living in the same house. One day he came home and wanted to talk. We had long since stopped sleeping together. I told him he wasn't permitted in our bedroom until I came out when ever he showed up at home. I agreed to talk to him and he said, "Jewel when I stay out at night I'm not out with the fellows, I'm out with a woman." I told Greg I knew that. I told him he needed to get his things out of the house because he wasn't paying anything there because all of his money was being smoked up, sniffed or sipped up. Greg was a drunk and drug addict. His family had hoped he had changed they said but you can see he didn't. He just hid his true self for as long as he could keep the farce going. He wanted to please his family but didn't really want to be saved. He was so bond and they were so tied up into themselves they couldn't see it. I prayed for his deliverance. One night I packed all his belongings and put them on the back porch. He stopped coming through our front door. Let me tell you this person was surprised! He kept knocking on our bedroom windows and telling me to let him in before he snapped. I rolled over and went to sleep. I had the locks changed that day so I wasn't worried about him coming in and hurting me. Greg was more self-destructive than anything else. I was so removed from him by now that we were really to people in a marriage that were so distant and absent from each other. We had no relationship because there was really no compatibility. I was just as miserable as he was being in the relationship. I was married but so lonely. My insides were screaming to be free. He didn't want to go home to his mom and I guess the other women wouldn't let him stay at their homes permanently. So I decided it was to my best interest to purchase a new place. I needed to be free of this mess.

I bought a house on the other side of town. I kept doing his mother's hair at my salon each week after work. I still attended his brother's church until one day his brother felt the need to tell me that Greg was seeing another one of my co-workers. Really this was one of the same women he was already seeing. It's strange because my school principal asked if I wanted their jobs. She said they could be fired for this inappropriate behavior. She said it made her sick. I told her "no." I felt everyone needs a job and he truly needed his and I wasn't going be the one to cause him to loose it. I wasn't going to act like a woman scorn. I walked those halls with my head held up. I smiled and spoke each time I saw them. Some days she would be in the lounge showing off what he had bought her and telling what she bought him. She was at least ten or fifteen years older. He wanted to be kept. He had married the wrong lady. She wanted an arm bracelet and he didn't mind being chosen. As I understand it she actually chased him.

I still went to all the family gatherings. They had helped me move my furniture into my new home. His family said they didn't want me caught up in his mess and hoped I would not go back or let him come to my home. I assured them that he would not be in my life ever again.

One Thursday before his mother's birthday she didn't show up for her hair appoint. She didn't call and when I called she didn't answer the phone. I left a message and she didn't return my call. Her birthday was that weekend and I was told not to come by Greg. I gave her a gift at church and she never parted her lips. I worshipped and praised God just as hard as they were. I felt if they could act like nothing had happened so could I. I hadn't done anything to them; or maybe I did? I had left their brother and maybe they really didn't believe it was over for me. Maybe they hoped I would take him back I really don't know what was going through their minds. I just know I continued serving in church until I knew it was time for me to leave. They would make smirks and silly remarks. They became distant and the more I stayed and served the angrier it seemed they became. One Sunday my sister-in-law told me not to act like things weren't bothering me. She said my praise wasn't real because she knew I had to be upset. She was wrong, very, very wrong! I was so free and God had given me a peace that not even I could understand. They were all acting funny. They continued treating me funny at church until I decided to leave. I relinquished all my duties and left.

Greg continued his wild behavior and needless to say, shortly after I left, he and the woman he was dating broke up. She said she was sorry she had ever got involved. She said she made a terrible mistake. We weren't together a year after we married. We were married in name only for two years.

I visited the church from time to time when invited by my niece and nephew. I would hear from his mother from time to time. One time while speaking to his mother I told her Greg said he wanted to try and get back together and her response was, "How long ago was that?" "It doesn't take a person a long time to do what he really wants to do if he wants it bad enough." She was right and my response to her was that I had already told her son I didn't want to be bothered and was happily divorced from him. I was surprised he had bothered to make the call.

Some years later Greg died due to his behavior. His family said he got saved before he died. I paid my respects when my niece called to tell me and stayed clear of them since. I must say that I'm glad he received Christ before he passed.

CHAPTER IV

Chattered Dreams and Broken Promises

I dated a surgeon not too long ago. I had just turned thirty-six and felt I had a better understanding of relationships. This man was highly intelligent saved and refreshing to converse with. He was tall with honey-suckle skin, sexy eyes, and a beautiful smile. His voice was so captivating and smooth it brought a euphoria effect all over you. Yes, the man was all of that and a bag of chips! He was not the boring nerdy type. I hardly got to see him because of his hectic schedule. He said we fit together like hand and glove. We could talk about anything. We found comfort in each other's company. We went to dinner, the movies and horseback riding when we could find time to see each other. We went to the symphony and enjoyed an opera one evening. We loved sports and would either go to college games, semi-pro games, and professional games or catch them on TV. One thing he didn't enjoy was board games. I love board games and I play chest but he wasn't game for any of this. But we found so many other things we had in common that his dislike of board games seemed trivial. We would get together and pray, read the bible and go to church some weekends. We kept it safe because we were too comfortable. Yes we were compatible! He was fun to be around. He would always tell me I was a breath of fresh air.

He had gone through a bitter divorce a year before we met and thought he was okay to start dating. I told him he needed to be sure and make sure he wasn't rebounding with me. Because he was the doctor he felt he knew what was best for him. I told him I felt he was suppressing his true emotions toward his break up and should put his thoughts into proper prospective. He was hiding behind his work and our relationship. We talked about this and he agreed to step back and take a closer look at his motive. He became very depressed during his time of soul searching and had an emotional break down and was hospitalized.

When he returned home he called and asked if he could come over, I said yes. He said he didn't know if I would be afraid to be around him. I told him I knew I had nothing to worry about. When he arrived on my doorstep I opened the door and ran into his arms. I gave him the biggest hug to reassure him that I felt safe with him being at my house. He wanted to review some scriptures and asked me to pray with him. He asked me if I would stick by him while he healed. I told him I would help him with his healing process. He saw it was getting late and knew it was time for him to leave. He turned to me and said I was easy to love and walked out the door. He would always tell me I was easy to love. Our relationship grew stronger. He took me to meet his mother. He invited me to go on a trip with him to the coast to secure his boat and meet a college classmate. He invited another college classmate along with himself to my house over the holidays. This was his best friend. This same best friend told him I was his wife. It all seemed so wonderful because we both seemed to want the same thing. It was so wonderful because for the first time in life I would have my dreams and promises come true! We spoke of marriage but I seemed to think we needed to take things slow because he wasn't quite ready for another marriage just yet. I wanted to be sure he was ready emotionally and spiritually. I was willing to wait however long it took.

I thought all was well and believe me it looked as if it was. Everyone said we made the perfect couple. They said we looked good together. Our relationship was peaceful, loving and pure. As he got better and stronger he started making excuses and start staying away from me more and more. He said he never had a relationship like ours before and that he felt he was backsliding. He said he never had anyone to pray and read the bible with in any of his other relationships. He said he was pulling back because he was falling deeper in love. He said he was going on a trip by himself and would see me when he got back. When he returned he gave me a call and told me he would pick me up from the school where I taught. I took my principal out to meet him. He had come to the school on a couple of occasions and while there asked to meet my principal and each time she was out of the building on another appointment. I felt this was a fine opportunity for them to meet. He smiled spoke and shook her hand and asked if I was ready to leave, I said yes and got into his car. The drive to my house seemed long and quiet. He answered my questions about his trip with short blunt lifeless expressions. He never looked at me while taking me home. I asked him why he was being short and distant. He said we would talk when we got in the house. When we arrive at my house he told me he was going to marry someone else and that he wasn't going to see me any more. He said he knew I was his wife but he had to do what was best for him. I was stunned because of all the promises he had made about us being together and all of my dreams of happiness.

He went away and married her and they are still together to this day. He came to me and told me he wasn't happy and knew he had done the wrong thing but didn't know what he could do to make it right. I told him I forgave him and asked him to forgive me for loving him. I told him I should have never fallen in love with him. I told him I wished him all the best and hoped he would be happy someday. He said she knew he didn't love her when he married her. He said she told him this and said he would grow to love her. He said he married her for all the wrong reasons, something he had told himself he would never do. He said he had married because he was in love the first time and that first wife had hurt him so badly he swore he would never marry for love again. So he got rid of me and married what he believed was best for him.

He was afraid to embrace our relationship because of a past experience and society. I had served my purpose by helping him. I was devastated for a while but soon realized he had done me a favor. To this day he tells friends he regrets his decision. My response is, "he made his choice."

CHAPTER

Blind Trust

Years have passed and I'm single, free and enjoying it! I'm in my late forties now and have lived this way for 12 years. I haven't had to worry about being bothered with anyone's drama. I've learned how to enjoy my own company. I've become in touch with the person I was truly meant to be. I'm happy with who I am. I have an inner peace. My happiness is not predicated upon circumstances, a man or any external situations. It comes from with in. A kind of happiness that comes from a person releasing crutches they formed through dependency on wrong things, subjects, and people that was passed on and taught from generation to generation. I had to have strong holds broken by God through prayer, faith, counseling, education and a strong determination to become a whole person. I had to learn balance in my personal life and in relationship. Yes, it's taken years but it's been worth it.

. I've been approached about dating but I've refused. I don't know why it's hard for people to believe a person can enjoy being single, celibate and free. Let me make myself clear. Celibacy is not easy; it takes a strong belief, constitution and will to be kept by the power of God! Besides girl, I choose not to be one of those women men use as a means of pleasure to get to their end; the real intended woman.

What is that old saying? "Why should he buy the cow when he can get the milk free!" Well, it won't be me. I know, I know, not all men are of this mindset. There are some genuine real trust worthy men out there somewhere if you can find them or hopefully pick them out from amongst the men on the down low. Nasty!

I know we weren't meant to live alone. I believe this to be a true fact, but I also believe that character, integrity, and compatibility is key to any real relationship and this seems to be the hardest challenge singles face. I'm not willing to take or put up with the crazy situations I found myself in during my twenties and half of my thirties. I've fought too long and hard; I've prayed far too many nights and days for the peace I've found. I'm reluctant to turn over my freedom to someone with no understanding of relationship, commitment, integrity, or just plain old morals. I believe that if God don't send him and let me know it, I don't want him.

I have a "blind trust" that God knows what's best for me and He'll present me as a rare gift; a hidden priceless treasure to the man that impress Him the most.

Hey! Besides I'm still single, celibate, and free to be me!